The Creative *Writer* for the Creative
NEWSPAPER

GIVE LOVE A CHANCE

TERENCE J. FRY

authorHOUSE®

AuthorHouse™ UK
1663 Liberty Drive
Bloomington, IN 47403 USA
www.authorhouse.co.uk
Phone: 0800.197.4150

Published by AuthorHouse 06/06/2017

ISBN: 978-1-5246-8213-2 (sc)
ISBN: 978-1-5246-8214-9 (hc)
ISBN: 978-1-5246-8220-0 (e)

Print information available on the last page.

CONTENTS

SYNOPSIS

As a young man of 16, the creative writer's mum and dad died in a car accident, and all he wanted to do, was to find out why the accident happened, and that lead him on a journey to becoming a journalist. In this story he falls in love with a woman who collapsed outside his house. She doesn't even know him yet. He visits her every day although she is in a comber, he is drawn closer and closer too her, and this gives him the determination to find out why she collapsed and to trace down the people that caused her injuries, this leads him to her university and an abortion clinic. He is determined to get his man when he finds out there are under-age abortions going on without the parents knowing anything about them, especially that the child is pregnant let alone going to the abortion clinic, he is determined to track down any of the clinics under age patients. He is lucky to be helped by a security guard. So the creative writer can give these families a chance to help their children through this very tough time in their lives and find piece in Christ, so they can forgive and be forgiven, for their past and for not being there as a family needs to be for each other, they find closure from Christ and help from the creative writer. This story has It's twist and turns. And there is a long journey to go on with an undercover cop involved.

FIND OUT IF THEY GET THEIR MAN.
AND MAY GOD-BLESS YOU.

CHAPTER 1

LOVE THY NEIGHBOUR

{CREATIVE Newspaper. 'TORNADO' HITS LEDGERS TOWN!}

The rain was pounding on the window, hard enough to break the glass, forcing it to crack, it began rattling furiously in the frame with the strength of the howling wind whirling round out side, it was howling louder as it sucked the glass right out of its frame and up into the twisting storm. As he looked out of the open window the creative writer noticed the people sat in their cars as this storm is passing through, they are trying to get out-of-town, and away from the tornado. As he looked through the broken window, watching the people outside.

The window frame of the other windows were rattling furiously and the glass was getting looser with every gust of wind.

He noticed all the people in the main road struggling against the wind. He thought what's with this weather, it's causing the hustle and bustle out there. The people were being blown furiously in and out of the road. One young man had been blown over and over again he went. Whilst people were being pushed and pulled to and fro by the wind, they were holding on to each other for stability. God bless! I'm glad I'm not out there, in that traffic sitting at a standstill. There are drivers furiously tooting at each other, they were getting wound up with the weather slowing

1

them down to a crawl. One man in a Jaguar car wound down his window, and shouted at the driver in front of him, {Not a good thing to do in this weather}? As he got a mouth full of rain, I chuckled to myself, the driver quickly shut his window, all this going on in a gale force wind it is ridiculous. He'd never seen so many people out on the street at all, they are panicking, running away from the storm!

The people that are queuing at the bus stop, are holding on to each other for stability. They look just like penguins shuffling around.

All this hassle just to get out-of-town, I don't know what they are thinking of. They should have stayed at home. That's the thing! If they still have a home? Maybe they should leave. He was listening to the radio and a news bulletin came on telling all the people evacuating from there homes to go to the Town hall, and the sports facility. There's so many people rushing around, no! That's not quite true! There is a funny bald man standing under the tree, and all he has is to protect himself with, is a pink financial newspaper, he is holding it over his head, it is flapping up and down in the wind slapping him on the head, it's not something I wouldn't recommend. I chuckled to myself as I thought of this man being slapped on the head with that socking wet newspaper! I burst out laughing! Laughing so loud, Gran could here him laughing in his office from the kitchen.

He carried on looking through the broken window he noticed a smartly dressed young women, she is struggling with her umbrella, fighting with it in the wind, he carried on laughing, she is holding it tightly but it is being pulled and pushed to and fro, he laughed so much that it made him cry! She tried to keep the umbrella up! It looked like a comedy sketch.

He thought she looked amazing with her wet curly brown hair, the way the rain dripped off her curls, and that deep red lipstick, with a shadow of blusher on her rosy pink cheeks. She was wearing a smart and stylish figure hugging pink overcoat that complimented her shape. Then he started looking at the finer details of what she was wearing. He closed his eyes drawing pictures in his head, as he recalled everything she was wearing, some gloves, a hat, and an umbrella all in a pale purple shade, however, he kept thinking of that umbrella, it just didn't do its job did it, as he laughed to himself, it got bent and twisted in the howling wind, making sure she got wetter than she would have done without it, he started chuckling, don't judge! Please don't! As he carried on laughing, it is her piece of treasure, and she refused to let it go at any cost. He was amazed at the appearance of her so amazing. He closed his eyes again and he could still see her with a fondness, it gave him a worrying feeling. He started thinking, I hope she's there tomorrow, I will go out and introduce my self and he took a second glance and saw she was clutching her stomach, he could see she was in extreme pain, it hurt him seeing her doubled over in pain. Was he meant to have feelings like this? Especially about someone he has never met before, he couldn't take his eyes of her, he couldn't stop himself feeling this way, as he was looking at her, his feelings were in turmoil, she was doubled over grabbing her stomach tightly, she was gasping for air, suddenly the creative writer felt a rush of despair, he started running out of his office, sliding on the banisters, down two flights of stairs{he had plenty of practice at that, as he was always getting told off by Gran.} He flung open the front door, it made a loud bang! And the wind started howling through the house, He desperately ran across the busy road. His Gran heard all the commotion and shouted from the kitchen, "What's all that noise about son?!" Thinking the front door glass had broken! She went to investigate and saw the chaos outside. So she went to the front door, and saw the creative writer putting himself in danger, she wondered why he would put himself in danger? What is he running across that main road for? Come to think of it, what is he doing out there at all, she said to herself, he's going to get himself killed! As he got to the other side, he bent down to help the young lady, she was nearly unconscious. Gran could see he was helping the young lady on the ground, it made her feel proud to see him doing that, to see her grandson helping someone he didn't even know!

The creative writer was shocked to see the other people walking past her, not-one person offering to help her. Gran thought why wouldn't the other passengers be bothered to get involved, she said to herself, he is there trying his best to help! Yet the other commuters just looked on oblivious to what was happening. Is the young lady invisible or something? What has happened to this world? The commuters were avoiding her like the plague, and they treated her like she is a drunk or worse, a drug addict! Although the women was barely conscious, the creative writer bent down and picked her up, he knew he had to get her to his home, to a safer place as fast as possible. He fought the wind and rain to cross the road, as the cars parted and time seamed to stand still, he was taken aback at the peace he felt all around him, the world carried on in slow motion. He knew he had her life in his hands, and something strange has just happened, while a man behind him clapped slowly and said "Good job man!" He thought to himself, What! Why couldn't that person have helped me instead of clapping. As he arrived at the front door exhausted with just enough breathe to shout, "Gran! Gran, help! Phone for an Ambu-la-nce!" Gran replied "It's already on its way son."

The creative writer was stood at the front door and shouted "Come in! Hurry up! Will you!" As they came through the door the paramedic asked, "Who needs help"? The creative writer said "Look! Just check her out, she needs your help! I don't know who she is! Just please, help her! She collapsed over the road. I saw her from my study up stairs". The paramedic checked her over, and saw some signs that she was bleeding, and put a drip in her arm. The paramedic was talking to the lady, reassuring her that everything would be fine. She went in and out of consciousness, the paramedics started shouting at her "You 'will' be okay!! Stay with me now!! Come on!! Stay with me!! Come on!!" they swiftly put her on the trolley and in to the ambulance. The creative writer definitely wanted to follow this story up, especially as not one person offered to help her, and he wanted to put the question to the world in the local paper.

WOULD YOU HELP YOUR NEIGHBOUR?

Would you help your neighbour, if they collapsed out side your house? If they clearly needed help? Maybe they collapsed, why wouldn't you help your neighbour? And why wouldn't you get involved? It's a life you could save. Just think how grateful they would be, and imagine how it would feel, to know you saved a life? Get involved and just think about how grateful there family will be. You will have a bond for life. {All these things are important to the creative writer}. So I ask you! "What has happened to our values?" if you wouldn't help them, why not? Supposing you was in trouble, wouldn't you want help from your neighbour? It came across his mind that he was following it up for selfish reasons, but he seemed at a loss as to what to do next. As he heard the ambulance going off with the sirens going and blue lights flashing! He started running towards the door, and shouted to his Gran, "I need to see if she is going to be OKAY! I am going to follow the ambulance to the Hospital, I won't be long Gran," "okay son" so Gran went to the front door to see him off. She was so proud of her grandson.

He jumped into his car and followed it closely, keeping as close to the ambulance as possible, {not that your meant to tailgate an ambulance}. He wanted to find out what was the cause of the young lady's problem's, although he felt he was intruding in her life. He really needed to know why she had collapsed? It felt like the story of his parents all over again, because he knew it would be on the! front page, of the morning paper, women collapsed in the high-street.

When he got to the hospital, he followed the paramedics pushing the trolley, he was so close too the paramedic team, you would think he was apart of the team, he was out of breath trying to keep up with the paramedics and doctors. All of a sudden a doctor stood right in front of him, and asked "if he was one of the family"? "No! I, I, I, I'm not! I just helped her". As he pointed towards the trolley he said "No I'm not!" "In that case stay here! Please! We will do all we can for her. What made you come to the hospital"? "I had to make sure she was going to be okay" "Why would you want to do that, and how do you know this patient?" "I told you I helped her! When I saw her collapse in the street, I brought her over to my house for safety. I couldn't just leave her there. Have you seen the damage the storm has done to this town? And you expected me to leave her out in that!? I couldn't stand by, and not doing anything to help her at all" The doctor realised by this time it was the towns very own creative writer.

The creative writer thought the doctor is in the wrong job. This Doctor has no heart! He wouldn't help someone that's collapsed in the road, so he replied to the doctor "I cannot stand by I can't do that! It's not me!" The doctor just shrugged his shoulders and replied "Well I think you are brave! Why would you take her into your house? After all you don't know her, do you"? " No I don't know her but I could see she needed help! Why, wouldn't you help her"? " Ho no, I can't take that risk out of this hospital!" "What risk do you mean? The risk of aids or that you will learn to actually care about someone"? The creative writer was getting mad with the doctors attitude, he was so selfish. The Doctor replied "Well you never know who you are taking into your home, do you!?" The creative writer said in a stern voice! "You don't know and wont know, unless you try helping someone out there, in the real world!" The doctor said "there are all sorts of people that would just con you in that type of situation". "What do you mean? Type of people? Type of situation!" It was obvious to the creative writer that the doctor really doesn't care about other people. He really thinks that someone would take advantage of the person that helped them. The creative writer said "I think it's a bit odd you saying that to me! You really think she will try to con me? Look at her doctor! She needs you more than you know! So you think on that! Doctor!! Do you really think that no one would want to get involved, in case they where conned"?! "No, but if they sued you, your in trouble! Wouldn't you say!" The creative writer thought to himself, that doctor is definitely insecure. The Doctor doesn't realise that you could make friends out of helping them, if you try, just try helping someone. After he thought for a moment the creative writer said "J would rather be sued for helping someone, and if it makes the papers, you should be proud of yourself, that you did what was right and was needed of you!" All this doctor thinks is rubbish! You may not know who you are helping, but you must help someone one day. The creative writer shouted "It's who I am! And what I do! That matters to me and my family!! What you think is wrong!!" This doctor obviously doesn't have empathy with his patients? He shouted "so why be a doctor, if your not going to care about your patients life?" By this time, I just wanted to know where the chapel is. I just to get some piece and quiet, I said "I'm sorry I've got to go, is there a chapel here?" the doctor asked "Why do you care so much about people you don't even know?" "It's very important to me to see a happy world. I'm an idealist, and I pray for many people that I don't even know, because I see them having some sort of trouble in there life. That's what being a Christian means! No one knows how many people are praying for them through there life". The doctor asks again "Have you seen this lady before?" "Only out of my study window, during the storm. I gazed out of the window watching the people being blown all over the place, and I don't know who she is, or where she comes from. It's the fact she needed help that matters!" By this time I was tiered and out of patients, I just wanted to know where the chapel is, just to get some piece and quiet. I had a splitting head ache by the time I got to the chapel of piece.

WHAT a palaver it was, to get the doctor to give me the directions to **THE CHAPEL OF PEACE**. As I opened the door to **THE CHAPEL OF PEACE.** I found it to be a small whitewashed cold room. With a big figure of Jesus at the front, on the table there was a dozen candles, lit in remembrance of someone prayer's to the lord. Ho boy it is tranquil in here. After I lit a candle and put some money on the table, I decided to sit on the wooden pew with a simple prayer book next to me. Although I didn't know the lady, I curiously looked in the book for some inspiration, while I sat praying and listening to god. I thought about the doctors, trying to save lives. Praying for the lord to help them and bring peace to their patients.

Then I went back to the waiting room. As I was walking backwards and forwards. I could hear the sound of my own feet pacing up and down, it sounded creepy, clip, clop, creek, creek, clip, clop, creek, creek. I kept asking every 5 minuets, "how the young lady was doing", the doctor was a little abrupt to me and said "She is stable!" It felt like hours had gone past, but it must have only been about an hour or so. I kept pestering the nurses trying to find out more, they consistently answered me with "She's stable for now", "what does that mean"? So I had to ask again, and again, I can't just sit here. "Excuse me may I asked what's really wrong with her? You just say 'stable for now' what is wrong with her? I need to know" " okay this will be a shock, not just to you, but she has had an abortion, and there seems to have been some complication". "Complication, how do you mean?" The doctor explained that the surgeon who performed this operation was either in a hurry, or incompetent. "I've seen a lot like this over the last two years", "two years", "Yes two years!" replies the doctor. "What can I do"? I asked "What can you do? When there's someone out there damaging these young girls". The doctor was disgusted that a surgeon could leave anyone with this damage, its plane and simple incompetence. The creative writer thought to himself, surly you can get pills to have abortions knower day's, I felt I needed to help the doctor, so I asked "what can I do to help you"? The doctor pauses for a minuet and said "Find out who the girl is! That is your first job! Are you not the one called THE CREATIVE WRITER for the local CREATIVE Newspaper?" "Yes"? "Well get ringing your editor and give him the story, to put it in to the paper, and publicise what a dangerous place, there is giving unscrupulous abortions to practically anyone, the girls that go to a place like that should think first, and go to there GP instead, or they will end up like this young lady here. Do you want that on your conscience"? "No!" "That's why you need to help today!" "Tell all the young girls to come to this hospital, we will help them as much as we can, with there familiar family problems. This is where they can get the best advice, and treatments. Can you 'just' do that"? "Yes I can do that! Can I take a photo for the paper, please"? "Yes, that's all right under these circumstances". When he went in to take the photo he couldn't believe all the tubes and sensor's that was on her body, she really was in a coma! It's a good job there is a nurse by her side watching the instruments panel. That's when he realised he really was in an intensive care unit. Not a pretty sight, there is 8 patients in the intensive care unit with 10 specialist nurses watching the monitors, for a sign, any sign, that the patient is getting better.

I left the intensive care unit traumatised, remembering what the doctor had said about being sued, for coursing more injuries to this young lady. My mind was going mad, I started hyperventilating, I just couldn't breathe! I kept telling my self to breathe, as all I could think about was the tubes connected to every part of her body, so when the doctor tried talking to me, I couldn't react in a natural way. I just walked right past the people that are trying to explain to me, what was going on in the room and why. I tried listening and understand the difficulties the patients are in, but couldn't, because I didn't now them, I knew my feelings were all over the place, and I was getting in too deep with my feelings for this particular young lady. I phoned my editor as soon as I came round, from the shock, of seeing these people with the tubes controlling there breathing, and machinery giving medication.

When the creative writer contacted the editor, he explained that this hospital has had a dozen women, that have had to come to the hospital, tragically because of bad abortions from a dangerous abortion clinic, after all they have been through {he needed to get his man}. It is my job to search out these fiends and to help bring them to justice.

Then the creative writer phoned his Gran to say the young lady was stable, and he would be home soon. "okay son, I'm getting tea ready soon" Gran knew he was hurting and wanted him to talk about it over tea "Okay Gran I won't be long". As he walked to his car he passed the coffee shop in the hospital gardens. He sighed ' ho yes! I need a cup of coffee, before I go anywhere' its been a stressful day. So he went in and to his surprise it was like a café book- shop, what a great place just to sit down and read a book with a coffee to unwind. He looked around the book shelves for ages to find a book to read, he found an old Romeo and Juliet, which is his favourite story of all time. He bought a coffee and a custard slice, so he had time to read, he seemed to lose himself in the book. The time flew by and the shop assistant was trying to close up, although he was oblivious to it all, she had cleared all the other tables, and mopped the floor, and even tapped him on the shoulder, he was so engrossed in the book, he hadn't heard her saying excuse me! I need to close up know! So she tapped him on the shoulder again, and kept repeating her self, thinking boy is he engrossed in this book, or just deaf, she shouted "excuse me its time to go!" He jumped up and was very apologetic and said "ho I'm sorry, I got lost in this book", "yes! I noticed, Its one of our finest books we have here". Gran was expecting him home for tea 2 hours a go.

As he walked in the back door to the kitchen, it showed on his face that he was still in shock, he couldn't think of anything ells, except the amount of tubes connected to the young lady, in the intensive care unit. At least the book gave him some me time Gran looked at him knowing he wasn't alright. He hasn't seen anything like that before. She said come on love, then he smiled, and thought about the coffee and custard, he had in the hospital café and went red, Gran knew there was something he wasn't telling her, she said "come on tell me what you've been up to young man", with that cheeky smile, I know you've been up to something, he smiled and said sorry Gran, I got engrossed in a book in the coffee shop at the hospital, it's a grand place to have some time out, I might go again and buy some books, as they collect for charity. She just laughed at him and said "that's okay you got embarrassed because of that, you do have a soft conscience". She laughed and laughed at him, the sight of his face then she quietly said "never mind that, how are you feeling about the young lady? Here have a cup of tea and tell me all about it, it will make you feel better you softy". "But I'm all right Gran", "you always get to involved with other peoples problems", "don't make a fuss Gran".

Gran thought about that morning and said "don't you think it is shocking that no one helped you with the young lady", "yes one of the doctors told me it's apparently down to the possibility they might get sued" "Sued! Who can sue you for helping to save there lives" "This world has got that way I'm afraid Gran" she replied "I would have given my right arm to have helped you with the young lady", "Unfortunately Gran that's not what you get knower days, it is people suing each other for nothing", Gran couldn't believe her ears.

He sat at the table waiting for his dinner to be taken out of the oven, as Gran was pouring the tea at that moment, he jokingly said, "can I have some beans on toast!" She went red and gave him a cold staring look, and took his dinner out of the oven, she nearly threw it at him, but he smiled and put his hands up and said " hay I was only joking, I do love your food Gran! And you of course, will you calm down Gran. What would I do without you Gran." "I don't know but you will be the death of me" then she gave him a clip around the ear, "Thanks Gran!" she just laughed. He thought it will be a funny memory, Being 25 years old and still getting a clip around the ear. They couldn't help themselves, laughing, at each other, just laughing, as he tried keeping a straight face Gran had her own ideas about keeping him amused, she started pulling funny faces, the type of face I was told not to pull when I was a child. He said Gran you are so funny when you pull that face, and he laughed hysterically. Gran stuck her tongue out and screwed her nose up at him again. He nearly chocked on his dinner, laughing that much, and struggling to breath between each laugh.

They started talking about the young lady, so he explained what the doctor had said, that she had an operation before, and that had gone wrong, he kept it simple so Gran wouldn't get upset. Being a Christian she doesn't believe in abortion's. He could see Gran was already getting upset at the thought of an abortion. He went over and gave her a cuddle, she smiled and said "thanks love I will be fine," I might go in to the office then? Instead of waiting for an answer, he jogged nervously up the stairs to the office. Thinking I better write some of this story up for the morning paper. His conscience wouldn't allow him to tell the whole story, he finds his conscience gets in the way of his job, so he went soul searching. Is it real writers block? No! Just a sign that his feelings are taking over. So he went to the living room. Gran looked at him and said "I can see Your heart is being pulled backward and forwards" Gran always knew what he was feeling. "No its okay," the creative writer and asked "Is it okay if I go in the office again?" "Yes of course son, you must get it right for the paper in the morning", he replied "I just want to do it better for her! Her story needs to be told, and that there are some unscrupulous people out there." Gran new he was in turmoil and said "you don't know what to tell the world do you son", "no Gran it feels to personal," As he always defines the truth with two sets of ideal's, from a victims point of view, or it's what they deserved to get, point of view. He did a lot of brain storming and wrote some notes for the story, his mind was in turmoil, how to give the true point of view?. His trust in Christ always wins the argument for the victim. He knows that life plays its hand, in everything you do, but you have to take some of the responsibility for your actions. That's what he is struggling with. Is it the women's fault, if she has an abortion and it goes wrong? Or is it the doctors fault? The doctor being incompetent and leaving her scared for life. That's what always plays on his conscience. He did his usual thing and worked on the conscience of the readers, to determine what they thought it would be like. He pointed out both sides of the story.

THE CREATIVE NEWS. A doctor makes mistake on the operating table. And a young women who didn't think she had any choice but to have an abortion, nearly bled to death. This young lady decided to have an abortion to help her self out of trouble. But she doesn't realise being pregnant is a gift from god.

He made sure that he told the public. That this adult female is in intensive care because of a stupid mistake, and that this has happened to twelve women, over the last 2 years. The local hospital has had to clean up the mess of a back street abortionist's.

When him and Gran got up that next morning and read the paper he saw It was front page news including the pictures THE CREATIVE NEWS, Girl looses blood on the high street, and nearly bleeds to death, nobody helps!

They asked people to contact the paper to try to find out who the woman is and pleaded to the public to trace her family, she needs her family by her side, but no one came forward to identify her.{is it because of shame or do the people really not know who she is. Don't they care}.

THE POLICE STATION. The next day he went to the locale police station to see if anyone with her description was reported missing, with no luck at the police station he felt gutted. The police made up posters and distributed them across the county. He felt drawn to the hospital, to see how she was getting on, he realised he still didn't know her name yet, someone must now her. Over the next few days, he popped in and out of the hospital as often as he could, just to see if she had come out of the coma, he stayed by her side as long as he could and as often as he could. He really was gutted, that this person nobody wants to identify. She is someone's daughter and lover. While he was sitting by the side of her bed and thought she might not make it to the next day. He started to write an obituary for the paper. He stopped himself thinking the worst! His heart yearned for her to wake up, if only to see her smile once {although the fact that she didn't know who he was didn't matter and she didn't even now he ever existed}. He was feeling hurt seeing her there in a coma, day in, day out, with the hope that only god could give him the answer. He prayed a simple prayer. Lord you give me hope when I need you, She needs you now! Please lord save her from any long term harm, amen. As he looked up at the nurse that was caring after her. He saw a spot of light and thought, what's that? He saw something, he knows he saw something out of the corner of his eye, there was an orb of bright white light shining around the young lady.

She opened her eyes! He realises what he had seen and was

significant in some way. The orb of light went around the nurse that was giving her a bed bath and she shouted, "she's waking up!" The creative writer felt ecstatic to here the good news, she is awake! Time to go over and introduce myself and ask who she is.

As the lady felt the cold soapy cloth on her skin, she screamed out loud "what are you doing to me!" "Its okay" said the nurse calmingly, "You needed a bed bath, so that's what I'm giving you, I will be done in a Mo". "where am I"? "You are in the intensive care unit, in the L.T.R.I". "I thought I was dreaming" the creative writer shouted "Doctor! Doctor! She's a wake!" Then he poised and gave a sigh of relief "can you find out who she is please? Its very important! I need to get her family here, to give her some support". "Yes! Yes!Yes! Just let me do my job" said the doctor. The young lady asked "what town am I in?" "Ledgers town" said the nurse. "Ho I thought I was at home", she started to shake and cry, she felt so alone and started asking why she was here in hospital. The nurse gave her a reassuring hand and said "calm down, we are here to help you, all we can".

The doctor took over and started to ask her questions "do you know you have lost the baby?" She started sobbing, "I had to do it", "do what?" The doctor asked, "have the abortion." The doctor felt sad for her, he said calmly, "no one has to have an abortion!" "but my family!" "What about your family"? She explained that her family didn't want her to come over to England. "Where are your family? He asked, "In NEW YORK. The USA". " What are you doing over here in England then"? "Are you on your own"? The creative writer shouted "Will you stop this infernal questioning"? You can see she is sobbing her hart out". But she answered anyway "yes!"

As the doctor was asking the questions for his report. The creative writer noted down all she said, but it felt wrong, it's the first time this job felt intrusive. I don't want to ask or write anything about this young lady, it felt like I had invaded her privacy.

As the doctor went on, she screamed out "what does any of this mater! I've lost the one thing I loved in this world, and that meant everything to me!" Tears are streaming down her face, she sat up and put her face in her hands and mumbled on saying "Although I wanted to be an architect, I wanted the baby more, but look at what I've done." the doctor said "You still can be an architect! You do realise, you may not be able to have children, because of the way the abortion was done". She started to scream with tears flooding down her face. She new it was all she wanted, and shouted out "I've always wanted children!" and screamed "I can't believe I blew my chances of becoming a mum!!" The doctor calmingly said "I didn't say that! I said you may have problems getting pregnant, so lets wait and see! Any way you haven't given us your name or address. We need to now who you are and how did you get to be like this". With tears streaming down her face she babbled out, "I went to a cheep abortionist". The creative writer noticed that this doctor really is sympathetic to her situation, as the doctor said " I now you are distressed, please let me help you, Is there anyone I can contact for you"? As she started to answer she began to lose consciousness, the doctor shouted to the nurse, "she's loosing consciousness again". The doctor went on and checked her blood pressure and pulse. And shouted to the nurse "Quick nurse! Get me some blood! She's got internal bleeding!" And they rushed her to the operating theatre. The creative writer didn't know what to do with himself, just as he was going to find out who she is, she was taken away to the operating theatre, but all he could do is to pray for her, after all she had no one ells here to do that. The creative writer poised and thought, she's been left in a mess, and just to think, it was all because of an abortion, that put her here! I need to follow this story up! Whatever mess this women young lady is in, I need to find out where she was operated on. He couldn't take the pressure and decided to go for a drive.

LEDGERS UNIVERSITY He found himself at ledgers town university, I must try to find out if anyone knows her here. The gates were open as he drove up he noticed the building's stature, it was an outstanding Edwardian building, it had huge double cast iron gates. As he drove up to the steps of the main entrance.

He thought to himself this is grand. The main entrance hall has wooden panelled walls. There was some large paintings of the founders of the university, there were pictures, pictures of all the Ledgers' Family Elders. It seamed a little conceited to him looking around the entrance. He asked at the front office where the head lecturers room was. The lady at the office started to show him the way, then he shouted "stop! Please stop and look at this photo! Can you tell me if you know her? I know you can't tell much from the picture, because of the tubes. But if so please help me! So I can tell her friends and family where she is"

The secretary started to gossip about the head lecturer, that he had employed at least one secretary a month. He is never satisfied, and tends to pick the lookers, that can't do the job, until about six months ago, when a secretary was employed, right up until last week. She just didn't turn up for work one day. So I think that she must be the young lady in you're a picture, and we've been looking for her too. The head lecturer is very fond of this one, he has had me ringing her every 5 minuets. The rummer is she got pregnant and split, I assume it's the same lady. "Ho Yes, I get it, I think!" Said the creative writer, hoping it was going to be the same person. He didn't like tittle tattle, but it was part of his job. Just think of a journalist that doesn't like being nosey, that's our man, and he only prints what he knows is true. "Who is she"? "I only know her as Kerry, there's a photo in her office, it's where we are going", "ho that's good". When they got to the secretary's office there was a temp sitting at the secretary's desk, so he impatiently asked if it was okay to go through her desk, to see if there are any clues as to who the missing secretary is. This woman is neat and tidy, so he thought, am I judging or looking at it objectively! The creative writer asked politely, "can we see the head lecturer, please"? You can tell him the creative writer is here from, the local paper, THE CREATIVE NEWSPAPER. "I'm here to help identify a young lady who is in hospital, I am hoping she is your missing secretary". "Just give me a minuet please", as the temp rang through and told the head lecturer that the creative writer wanted to see him, she was interrupted by the creative writer, he shouted "It's about a young-lady that's in hospital!! " As the secretary blushed she said "go straight in". As they went in, the head lecturer stood up from his desk and said "good morning I'm the head, what can I do for you"? "Can you look at this photo please, and tell me if you know her"? "she looks familiar but no I don't think so". I have had secretary problems for some time. The one that's gone missing I've had for six months. I'm worried she is hurt and stuck somewhere, she is so dependable, so I've tried phoning her home and mobile phone, the mobile said "please leave a message, sorry unavailable ..."

The creative writer asked "Is it okay if I look through her desk, to find out where she has gone to"? "Yes that's okay", "What is her name"? "she's called Kerrie". The creative writer said he wanted her to be called a mystery receptionist in the paper, "if that's okay"? "Yes that's fine" replied the lecturer. "great, I will get it put in to the paper tomorrow". So they went in to the receptionists' office and the creative writer asked "Can we get to this desk please? Come on I haven't got all day!" The creative writer said hastily, "yes I know that"! Replied the secretary, who was so embarrassed by his abruptness, he replies "Sorry its been a long day". And he went through the secretary's desk and found two Passports, both with the same pictures, but different names and both out of date, a mercury switch, some pieces of wire, a soldering ion, solder and a receipt for a walking talking dole. He shouted to the secretary, "I think you better get the police down here, right away!!" The creative writer got all the peoples names that new the missing secretary, so he could follow this story through to the end, he got rather excited at the thought of chasing down this young filly, as he thinks she is a terrorist? He thought what a warped mined she must have, to be a terrorist, in this time of piece, throughout the land of the Christian world. Everybody that knew her was shocked at what was found. The temp phoned 999 and asked for the Police and told the controller there is a woman that's been missing for a week and a half, and two passports have been found with her photo in, with two different names, one is in the name of Kerrie Hamilton, and the other one in the name of Kerrie Gerald.

The police told them to keep away from the desk, so they can send a specialised investigating team, to see what can be found out about the suspected terrorist, missing secretary. While the police were on there way to the university, they told the creative writer to leave everything alone, because she is a terrorist. The creative writer was on the case! But got stopped in his tracks, because it's a terrorist enquiry. They explicitly told him to keep away from the desk.{that was a bit late, he has been all over it with a fine tooth comb}

The police finally arrived a little after six o'clock, they kept us there for an hour to ask what we knew of the suspect. They also went through the secretary's desk and found a package glued to the underside of the middle draw. While one policemen was searching for prints, another bagged up the

Passports, the mercury switch and bits of wire, and of course the mystery package, ho and the soldering iron. They also swabbed the desk for residues of explosives, which was positive, The creative writer noticed the policemen that had bagging up the evidence forgot the receipt for the doll, and the creative writer said "Excuse me you've forgotten something, the receipt! Don't you need it". The special officer wasn't impressed with my attitude, but it was now getting late and I / we just wanted go home. They also found some other prints in the office that connected other terrorist's suspects to the case, this proved, she was in a terrorist network and not working on her own. They have been using the university's office as a base. I thought the science lab should be checked out, but when I suggested it, the police were very indignant they knew exactly what they were looking for.

While the creative writer was taking notes of all the commotion, the lecturer was being interviewed by the terrorist special forces officer, and the police had decided to take all of us to the police station for more questioning. The creative writer wasn't impressed, he hated the cells at the best of times, and to his surprise, he was let go with in the first hour, without being interviewed, which he thought a little strange, and noted it down in his book. He asked if he is allowed to tell the paper about the possibility of a terrorist attack in ledgers town, or there are terrorist's in the ledger town area. But the police put a lid on it, as she has been in hiding for 10 days, they didn't want anyone to spook her away from the area. The police already have locations she turns up at regular times in the day, and that's the end of that one for know! But you never know what the future brings. I will not let go of it altogether. THE CREATIVE **NEWS reports, INTERNAL BLEEDING IS FOUND AS COMA PATIENT WAKES UP!**

The doctors lack of intuition to find a damaged internal organ, caused a young lady to be rushed back into surgery after just coming around from a coma, that must have been apparent to the doctors at the time of there original operation to help this young lady, but thought it wasn't necessary to investigate any further. Was it a mistake of the surgeon that repaired her apparent abortion wound? Or was it the surgeon that missed a stitch as they repaired her from the initial bleeding? We need to have an investigation in to the surgeon that missed the damaged organ! Causing it to bleed profusely again when she had woken up from the coma.

THE SECURITY OFFICE. The next morning the creative writer went back to the university hoping to find out who the lady is in hospital. As he had got court up in the terrorist investigation by the police yesterday. He went to the head lecturers' office to asked if they had a security ID sections in the university. The head lecturer said "we have all our girls ID's on the security computer, in the security office". He was a little over whelmed, by all the attention the university had got in the last couple of days, and directed Miss Smith the receptionist at the front desk, to help me go through all the relevant security files and photographs, as we walked to the security office the chit chat was about the young lady in hospital, and she asked "what colour hair," "Brown curly hair, long legs, short body," "you've got a good memory." Boy did I get embarrassed thinking I've been seeing her long enough to be able to draw her with my eyes closed, " ho yes small hands", "a very pretty looking young lady then", "ho yes! And beautiful brown eyes". "The description rings a bell, but I can't put a name to it." They got to the security office and started looking through the security paperwork, it was hours before they got a hit, with the name Jacky-May. He said "that's a funny name isn't it", "yes I've only heard of a song with that name" "yer me too". The creative writer needed to take a walk, it has been a hard day stuck in a stuffy office, and he said "can I take a walk around the university, Just to get a feel of the place", "yes that's no problem, here put this badge on, so people know who you are", then she spoke in a sad voice "I do hope we find out how to contact her family," he replied "we don't have any next of kin in this country, they are all international telephone-numbers". "Yes I noticed, so lets try ringing all the numbers given on the entrance form before you go for your walk", they all seem to be discontinued phone numbers. He realised this lady didn't want anyone to know who she is! That put him in a frame of mined to try harder, why didn't she want anyone to know who she is? He wasn't giving up on this story, although it was going nowhere fast. He expected to make a breakthrough any day soon. He said politely "okay thanks and god bless you, for all your help with the information." "Ho that's okay, see you soon I hope," said the receptionist as she flirted with him.

He went for a walk around the university and while in the university car park, he noticed one of the boys looking at him suspiciously, he wasn't thinking about the crowd of people there. As he looked up at that one particular boy, he stood out from the rest of them. They looked at each other across the car park, the boy then turned around and whispered to the others in the group, so the creative writer called the lad over and showed him the photo, and asked the boy if he knew her, the boy went red and said you must have the wrong place mate, "she's not from around here mate". "Mate is that how they teach you to speak here"? The lad went red as a beetroot, that made the creative writer think he was on to a winner, yes! Someone that actually knows her, Yes! Yes! Yes! And started skipping. Then he watched the lad intensely, as he returned over to the crowed, they all laughed and hugged around in a circle whispering and looking back over at the creative writer with drawn daggers, they shouted over to him, "yer mate you've got the wrong place". He realised he wasn't going to get anything out of them. So he just sat on the bonnet of his car, contemplating his next move and wrote some notes down for the paper. Then he noticed a couple of the girls getting upset and run off from the crowd, he decided to see where the girls where going to. He followed them around to the track and field course, although they were upset they were getting ready for the training races, for the county trials. They started warming up with the rest of the team, doing the exercises and meditation or concentration exercises. As he approached the edge of the track the two girls looked over and whispered to each other, they came over to get a towel out of the team bag, and they stood about 1m away from him while speaking in a lowish voice to him, saying they couldn't help right now. But to meet them in the café in the high street THE LITTLE TOTTERS CAFÉ AND WINE BAR.

He noticed a young man training his hart out. He was by far the fastest runner at the track, this gave the creative writer another story- THE FASTEST RUNNER IN TOWN. He went over to introduce himself, "high I'm the creative writer what's your name"? " I'm Colin Grady" he interviews the young man about his training regime, and especially what he eats, the young man explained he had a specialised diet, it is a high protein diet supplemented with vitamins and shakes, I asked who provided the vitamins and it turned out it was all run from the universities sports training program, and scientist's, I then asked how controlling they where, the runner said "its hard than I expected it to be, the way it is", because he believes in the people and the program they run here. The creative writer asked to see this type of vitamins and shakes, he went over to his bag and got out what looked like a way protean shake and some vitamin pills.

Colin Grady agreed to allow THE CREATIVE WRITER around to his home and for a training session, they agreed to meet later that week, he couldn't wait!

Chapter 2

The Hunt For The Family

The creative writer decided to try the town centre for any other leads. As he showed the market traders the photo and was explaining what had happened to this young lady. It was like hitting his head on a brick wall. Then he saw the café and went in to browse around, although he wasn't expecting the girls from the track and field team to turn up till much later. He went to the bar and ordered a drink. He took a good look around, it was pretty snazzy, and in a classic styled café wine bar style. There was red leathered swivel stools with high quality chrome, and a highly polished red shelf around the wall, with a mirror all around, and black tables with white crocheted table cloths. The way they were set out it made it look stunning, a youngsters type of café, Boy did he stand out like a saw thumb, it began to pack out with uni students, with there long hair and ripped jeans, wow ripped jeans are back in. What am I doing here I'm nuts being in a bar like this. Just as he was going to leave a couple of the young men recognised him, and came over to asked what he was up to, "I'm interested in finding the family of a young lady, she nearly died in hospital and needs them at her side." As he hadn't been to the café before he was a bit weary, but the lads where interested in the things he loved to talk about. They talked about the runner, how fast he is and how much faster they think he will be in a years time at the Olympic try outs, They argued about how good he was because of the lack of determination, and the additives he uses. They were really interested in journalism and have taken it as one of there studies, they loved interviewing people but hated the writing bit. "Well you know I'm actually working on a story now, and I am after some information on a young women". "She collapsed in the main street outside my house, I won't tell you exactly where on the main street, I don't think my Gran would appreciate every one coming round", "you mean we can't come round and chill-out with you", he laughed, and said "you could if you wanted to, lets get to know each other a bit better first, I will help you with your reports and for a newspaper". The lad boasted "lets see if we can actually get it in print", "it will be good for your grades at the end of the course. You could pick up a story anywhere. Hay back to the woman I want to find out about especially where I can find her family, She is in a pretty bad way", "I see," "what's wrong with her"? Said one of the students "That's privileged information sorry, well lets just say she was in the intensive care unit. This is a picture of her", "yes we know her! She's defiantly one from the uni, but I can't remember what her name is she's not in any of my studies you see". "I do know she has a flat nearby, but that's about all we know". One of them suggested the reason he thinks she is in the hospital, is something to do with drugs? "why!? Do you know of any drug dealers that are around"? "Hay sorry were not in to that sort of thing, but you can see the big built man in the corner, we know he has parties every weekend, he once went out with her", "and there's always some drugs available at his party's","What do you mean available". "There is a table with the drugs on a tray to try out!" "It is to get you hooked, you mean! So they can take your money and your dignity too!". "We're too scared to try them, as we see what happens to the people that are taking them". "There all over the place, we get out before it gets to bad". "what do you mean to bad"? "There's plenty of people that always get smashed and ends up in the bed rooms", "I get the message! Why do you leave before the sex starts? Your students! Don't students usually try this stuff out first"? "We want to stand up and to be counted, we don't need that type of entertainment, and we are saving the sex for our wedding night". "That's pretty noble of you".he started laughing but they just stared at him, they didn't realise what he was laughing about, he said you two are getting married! They were so embarrassed but couldn't do anything ells but laugh themselves. "I didn't expect that answer from people of your age. I'm so impressed, you do mean the two girls over there? May you keep that in your hart until you are on your wedding night? Are you Christians"? "yer we go to the baptist church down the high street, St Peters. It starts with prayers at 9 O clock". "Would you mind if I came Sunday?" "No it will be a pleasure" "thank you, I would love to go. That is somewhere I could take my Gran." "Only if she likes a rocking, raving church." "Just one more thing can you get me the name of him over there, so I can do some investigating" "well I, I don't know about that, I think we've given you too much information as it is!" "Did you say you where Christians and wanted to be reporters?" "Okay you got us there," we will get it for you! They went over to there girlfriends, and a friend of a friend, knew who he was. He came back to the creative writer and said "His name is Jordan", "okay thanks for that." {I think I will see how many (Jordan's) there are here in the town seances, to see if he is a serious drug dealer? I need to go to the police records}. The students asked the creative writer one more thing in exchange, "ha, ha, ha. Have you got a case you was working on, I can use as my essay?" "Well! Yes! Look into your head lecturer, I here he has some shenanigan, s going on with his secretaries", "Yes we will let you know what we find out", "I'm not bothered about that, but you can still find out, and do your essay on the lecturer and especially if you get it in to the paper, but make sure what you get printed by the paper is true." So the creative writer said "Ho yes one more thing I'm guessing you tell me if there's a teacher after the girls". "Yes there is a teacher all the girls are after", "it's a rummer he's got a few pregnant, and they left, the good looking girls keep dropping out of his classes". "Are you sure your not just jealous?" "Now because you know this are our girls! Christians, true Christians, we are not like most people". "them Over there!" The girls where scantily dressed! Wearing very short Minnie skirts, if that's what they are. Not really a skirt at all, a wide belt, I would call them, I should really calm down know LOL and he said "I thought you was Christians," " we are! They are to. It's not what you wear, that makes you a Christian, but asking the love of Christ in to your life!" "okay you got me there." The girls smiled and waved at him. He smiled and thought, boy has church changed, since I was a choir boy.

The lads said to the creative writer, "Our girls aren't good enough for that teacher. He likes the posh looking ones, not that he's got a chance with ours anyway!" "What do you mean"? "They are Christians to that's why", "What's the name of the teacher"? He also thought what's the name of this church LoL, the girls are something, "the teachers name is DR Duncan Butterfield, he teaches design engineering, he has a doctorate in Building engineering. All the. A Class students are in his lectures." "what's your two names?" "I'm Kenny and this is Thomas", why are you both in uni, and not out there trying to get a job as a reporter or journalist? I'm sure there are some small papers still looking for good journalists! "Well were here for the good life, learning a bit and checkout the chicks! Ho! No I'm only joking! We want to be a journalist like you, but we find it hard to follow up the stories". "Yes its harder than it looks", "how do you do it day in day out"? "You could just follow the leads, sometimes it's all there is! You just need to connect the dots together, and that's what you need to put into practice, to put it into the right context, organise it and format it properly. You could make a story out of your own life in uni, call it a week in the life of a student, or you could do a story on meeting me, and follow it up by looking in the old papers, find out what I've written about, do your research! To be a journalist please concentrate on your essay's and not do too much high living, never assume anything! Just follow the leads properly and you can find out the truth". "All story's have 2 sides to write about. The good someone does in there life, and what happened to change them in there life to make them a cynical person."

As the two boys where talking to the creative writer, the

track and field team came in, and the two girls he had spoken to before were with them. They blushed and giggled a bit as they went passed him to the bar. They said hi to the two boys. While the track and field team were getting served at the bar the two girls came over to talk to the three of us. One whispered in my ear, "this is a good cover to talk to you about Jacky-May, the girl in your picture, with these 2 other students here!" They joined in with the conversations. Then they explained to him things they saw in Jacky-May. He was stunned and said "did you say Jacky-May"? {conformation her name is Jacky-May} "yes that's her name! We think"? And they explained the way she was with the other students! Such a and polite, always helpful to fellow students. If they where behind with there studies she helped them catch up. The fellow students can't believe she is in hospital because of an abortion, she didn't seem the type to do that, or more to the point, she didn't look pregnant at all? That raises questions about what happened to her? They had confirmed that she was in a relationship with the teacher, and started to open up with him. They also told him about a flat she had in town, and they thought she was doing some modelling work for one of the local photographers. She had the flat at the market place near all the café, s wine bars and restaurants. She was frequently seeing Mr Butterfield. The creative writer found out that most of the student's came into town most nights, no surprise there then! In there opinion it seamed as though Dr Butterfield and the young lady where good friends. I thought I had enough to drink by now, so I told them I was ready to go, and ask them if I could contact them again, and said "you don't know how much you have helped me thank you. Here have a drink on me." As he began to leave one of the girls slipped a piece of paper in his hand, Ho that was unexpected he thought. I hope it is a good lead to finding out how Jacky-May got in this mess.

The next day the Creative Writer tried finding out who was dealing in drugs on campus, and whether that was anything to do with why she ended up pregnant, and having the abortion? Or was it the teacher that was the father from the beginning?

On the piece of paper that he was given, was a couple of names, Jordan-Butterfield and Jack McGregor. He ran the names through known drug dealers in the local police station. They both seem to have had plenty to do with drugs! But when it went to court nothing seemed to stick. They always got off on a technicality, or the evidence disappeared? They defiantly have some connections in the right places! The creative writer thought to himself this is amazing, I only wanted to finish of one story, and I've got another three at least, plenty of work for the future, back to Jacky-May. Although Jacky-May was an acquaintance, there's no evidence leading to Jacky-May and drugs not yet any way. My question to the world is, why do people go to back street abortionist's? There's a beautiful hospital here, the L.T.R.I. Why didn't they or Jacky-May just come here instead of the back street abortionist.

THE TORNADO UPDATE. During the tornado, a woman that had collapse at the bus stop, everybody was so taken up with looking after their own needs they just didn't bother to help. But thanks to our own raving reporter, she was taken to hospital and is doing fine! As the tornado hit the TOWN OF LEDGERS. There was a lot of business casualties one of them was the roof being ripped off the local car factory, and it will take two months to put the factory beck into production of our famous sports cars to be in production again. There is plenty of work for the local builders too, as chimney pots fell by the dozen all over the town, And well I don't think there is a fence left standing in the town. The whole side of one house was ripped down and roof's being ripped off by the dozen. The casualties so far are 154 injured and 2 dead due to the tornado. We have a fine town to get back into tip top condition before the, T, T, trustee comes through the town later next month, we must make sure its ready for the **TT racing** to start this summer. **Are we all ready to tidy up this town.**

Yours thankfully, **THE CREATIVE WRITER**

The next morning the creative writer went around town trying to find out whether the lady had been seen on the day she collapsed, its been nearly a week know, all I know is her name Jacky-May.

He asked all the market stall holders, if anyone knew the girl called Jacky-May. It seamed she loves the fresh fruit, every morning she would buy a banana, apple, and peach, from one particular trader. He explained she was always polite happy and a caring person. "She had a black brief case with her earlier on the day she collapsed", said the fruit stall trader. But there was no briefcase when she collapsed outside my house.{ha a brief case to find?} The creative writer explained to the stall holders what had happened to Jacky-May, and she was in hospital. It took all day and he still had no luck, except from the stall holder that sold her lunch.

The creative writer could feel he was being followed, as he turned around, at first sight he didn't notice anything out of the ordinary, but at a second look, he noticed two distinguished looking men in fine mohair overcoat's, slowly moving towards him. They kept looking in the windows at a strange angle, one on each side of the road. That's how he knew they were looking at him and every move he made they made. Yes it was strange enough to look suspicious.

He had a rushed of blood to the head and panic struck him-down, he has never been panicked by anyone before, he thought I need to get out of here, I'm feelings stifled {The pressure was building up in him}. How can I get away from these people?! Just at that moment an open back double decker bus went past, and he made a run for it, he ran as fast as could, then with a big jump, he landed with a big bang as he bumped in to the bus conductor. With excitement he shouted "Yes! Oh yes! I just made it!" {he was dancing for joy}. "That's my boy!" Said the conductor "fares please," "ho I don't know where I'm going to yet". That will be £2.30" right to the end then". The creative writer said "sorry I bumped into you," {the creative writer had a little laugh to him self. He was grinning from ear to ear} "That's okay come on! Get in the bus, where are you going to be safe". "Ho I better get to the hospital". The conductor continued talking over him, "I'm used to people jumping on the bus around here", "What do you mean!","well let's just say there's always someone running from someone around here? It's a bad area you now!" "So what are you running from"? "That's a very good question? I have no idea but you see them men over there? The men running towards a jag" "yes I see", "what did you do to get them chasing you around town"? "I told you nothing!" "Well it must be something","No It's not! What are you a bus conductor or a journalist?!" he had to laugh he was thinking I'm the journalist. "Well it's your lucky day! Look they're fumbling with their keys, hay your home free!". By the time they got sorted out with the keys the bus was out of site, and It was too late for them to catch him up. As he had got away from who knows what! All he knows is that someone is rattled with him being in the town, and asking questions about Jacky-May the young lady in hospital?

The conductor said "Well boy you can say that was close" "yes that's true but I've got to get back to the hospital. I haven't got much time and I haven't a clue where this bus goes". The conductor continues talking, babbling on, then he realised what the creative writer said and shouted "okay!!! "so loud it hurt his ears, as if to tell someone else. After just being chased the creative writer got a little spooked and studied the people on the bus, he thought there must be a reason to shout so loud maybe its just a coincidence then he noticed there was an old man with a grey moustache that looked out-of-place, he was wearying a smart grey overcoat and a grey trilby hat, with a brown band around it, he is posh and no way needed to use a bus, what is his story, you could see he even had his hands manicured, I would like to know his story. Then the conductor shouted "it's the hospital you want then?" "Yes please," "I will tell you where to go when you get off the bus, is that okay!". "Yes thank you"{it was only two more stops around the corner, when he was told to get off the bus}. The conductor told him the way to the hospital, "its just around the corner, across the road, go through the park and your there. The hospital is right in front of you." As he got off the bus he notices the old man got up to get off too, he could see the hospital building and he ran across the road and through the park to the hospital, just as he got out of sight of the old man. When he got to the hospital gates, he saw the men that was following him around town, they are in the jag leaving the hospital car park. The creative writer thought that's it, its got to be something to do with the lady in the hospital. What's so special about that women? Jacky-May! What would Someone put a tag on me for? Because I am trying to find out what happened to Jacky-May. Why are they worried about what I might find out. Questions! Questions! Questions! And more questions. I know what I've found out! And that's not a lot {ha the brief case} what's the missing brief case got to do with it? And there's the possibility Jacky-May has crossed someone ells, as he was contemplating all these things the old man was catching him up at a determined rate, who is he? And the two men in a jag following my every move down that high street? They looked like gangsters with class! Well I suppose I will have to put them on hold for the moment, just until I can get some answers from Jacky-may.

He thought he better get her some juice as the water in the hospital isn't very good on its own, it has the infernal taste of chlorine and sewage minus the bacteria.

CHAPTER 3

COLIN VISITS, JACKY-MAY

When he got to the hospital, he asked at the desk what ward Jacky-May is on. The security guard looked through the computer and said "we don't have a Jacky-May on the list sorry!" he thought they had got to Jacky-May and started arguing with the security guard at the desk, "But I know she is here!!" he explained "I followed the ambulance here and talked to the doctors earlier, you can't loose a patient in the hospital can you"? The assistant at the desk shrugged his shoulders and then asked, "are you a relative", "no, just a friend", "well I can't help you sorry," then he saw it come up on the computer and couldn't help himself, and blurted out, "ha its just come up, she's been put in to ward nine", "okay, thank you!" Hang on, I haven't phoned them with her name yet? Somebody ells must have given her name to you. Another question to be answered? "Excuse me what way is ward nine please"? "Down the corridor to the end, turn right, the wards on the left." "okay thank you".

He was looking for the ward office when a nurse popped out of a side room, and boy did he jump, feeling nervous he said "Ho, can you tell me who Jacky-May is?" "She's doing fine and I would like to say, she is going to be running around within a couple of days, but I don't think that will be happening any time soon". "Ha can I ask you how you found out her name? I've not long known it myself", "Ho yesterday, we had a visitor that identified her. She will be very sore for about a week so take it easy with her". "Can you tell me whether it was a man or woman"? "woman or I should say 2 women, they said you saw them at the café" "ha, got it now, I know who you mean!" "What about the internal bleeding, what was it? Why didn't you notice it before she collapsed"? The nurse went bright red and replied with, "I'm sorry I cannot tell you anything else, but she's going to be alright, we caught the internal bleeding just in time. You are very lucky to have her here". "How, am I? Thank you. Why did you say that"? "Well she has had the best surgeon in the country doing the operation, that's what you call very lucky in her case." "Who is the doctor that's looking after her" "He is a surgeon, Mr Ivan Roberts, he is looking after her needs." "Hah can I go in and see her now?" "Yes", "what room is she in?" "It is the room over there, no.3".

When he got to the room he saw her in bed 4, she was just coming around. There was a doctor giving her a check over, he kept saying to him self, hmm, hmm. The creative writer walked in and said "can I talk to her doctor please?" "Yes that's fine, are you family? Because she needs all the help she can get", "No, just a friend". As he walked towards the bed she looked up at him in a very strange squinted way. "Hi my names" he poised and said " ho this is a little awkward, I guess your wandering why a stranger is coming to see you", "Yes! Who are you?" " I'm Colin, Colin-forester, I'm covering your story for selfish reasons. I am a reporter by trade and well you just happen to come in to my life during the storm, you see I was the one that helped you when you collapsed. I just picked you up from the bus stop, outside my house". "O sorry that sounded wrong!" She smiled at him thinking he's a little clumsy with his words. "That's a good sign!" Said the doctor, "What is" asked Colin, "to see her smiling"

"They just wanted me to marry the son of a friend of the family, he is like a brother to me, not anything ells". "Come on this isn't the time to be thinking about that know. I will get you a tablet to calm you down, so you can rest tonight". Jacky-May was sweating with worry! Wile the nurse wiped her brow with a cool damp cloth she said in a calming voice, "here take this, it will relax you", as she handed her a tablet. "We will talk about it in the morning, only if you want to that is," "I'm not sure I want to yet, thanks anyway" "I'm just going off duty, I will see you in the morning".

In the meantime, Colin had gone straight home, and as he walked in the side door to the kitchen, he called his Gran with cheer in his voice, "I'm home, do you want a cup of tea making"? " please dear, I like your tea!" "and why is that Gran". "It always taste better when you make it". " you do make me laugh Gran. Hey Gran you know that women in hospital", " you can tell her name, if you want to", "okay Gran her names Jacky-May! She is quite sweet, she had her final operation today, she is so easy to talk to, I'm going to see her at around 7ish, you don't mind do you Gran?", "now that's fine, you go, talk to your new love", "It's not like that Gran", "I can see it in yours eyes and here it in your voice son, you really like her don't you". "Yes Gran I think so. Can we have plain egg and chips for tea Gran?" "as long as you're cooking", "okay I will look after you tonight Gran". Colin only cooks when he has friends round for a dinner party, but never when he's just come home from an interview.

Colin couldn't wait to go back to the hospital, he was so excited his hart was jumping hoops, and he spent the rest of that evening waiting for the time to get to 6.30, to help time pass he started looking up the names on the piece of paper he got from the girl at the café bar, Jordan Butterfield and jack McGregor, wile he was on his laptop. He found out that Jordan Butterfield was a cousin of Mr/Dr Butterfield and jack McGregor was a distant cousin. Colin thought can we find out if the two Butterfield's and McGregor are in to the drug dealing in the university, I know Jordan Butterfield is in to drugs. Ha, the briefcase! Was there drugs in the briefcase? I don't think so, she's not that type of person, Or could they have been using Jacky-May? His mind was doing overtime. Did Jacky-May just get in the way? Or did she over hear something she shouldn't have? Was it just the temptation of drug's in what she thought would be a safe place,? A safe place that made it so tempting with people you trust {It seems I'm getting more questions than answers}. And the old man, he knew where to bring the flowers, Of course you silly sausage, it was the newspaper.

Colin decided to go in early that evening, to ask Jacky-May some question's about her family. He was sweating with nervous anticipation, he wanted to see her beautiful rosy cheeks and exceptionally beautiful big brown eyes. As he walked in the nurse told him "not to disturb her, as she had not had any sleep all day, and needs her rest". Jacky-May over heard the nurse and looked over to the door, she could see Colin leaving, he looked dejected, she shouted "no don't go! I want to tell you what happened". Colin couldn't resist her demand and he turned back towards her room, "Well OK, only if you want to" he replied, are you really ready to tell me what happened. "Yes of course I will. Then before you start," Colin was interrupted by the nurse, "I thought I told you to go and leave her to get some sleep! "Ho OK! "I don't think we are going to get that chat after all" said Colin. "Please nurse I want him to stay, it's OK nurse! I can cope, I'm feeling much, much, better than I was earlier", "OK if you really want to talk to Colin our famous roving reporter", she said it with a smile on her face. "Colin take it easy on her, she's not well at all". "OK I will I promise". Colin made her take a deep relaxing breath before they started, "know tell me what you want to tell me, but I have lots of questions I would like to ask later is that okay" "well-yes? O boy, where do I start, I was going out with what one would call a bad boy, for about 6 months he was always sweet to me, until I got pregnant, then he didn't want to now me at all. He left me on my own being pregnant, and without anything, not even a forwarding address, I don't know the area very well. You see don't you, I felt used! So I decided to carry on and have the baby. I didn't think I could afford the flat in the centre of town. I can't get in touch with him, not even if I wanted to, because the town centre is all I know. Then about two months went by and a teacher took some interest in me, I was flattered in my condition, I didn't expect anyone to be interested in me? We decided to have a few meals together, he made me laugh, and it was quit a shock to find myself attracted to a 30 something man. He has been treating me well, up until before the abortion". This week?" "you mean last week". "Has it been that long since I came in to hospital"? "Yes you have been here nearly 2 weeks". "O boy! You are giving me a scare, any way, Dr Butterfield the professor of building design technology, and I, had been going out as friends for about two weeks. I felt I could trust him, and I had decided to have the baby, he tried talking me in to giving up the baby, you see I thought, I needed to follow my career, and do my modelling, to pay for my flat and uni fees, but him and one of my friends jack McGregor, talked me in to having an abortion, they organised it for me. Just after the operation to get rid of the baby, I had realised they worked me like a pro". "what do you mean?" "I found out they where brothers, Jordan Butterfield and Dr Butterfield", "I see, that must be very distressing for you, to find that out"? "Yes it was, so I talked to my other friend jack, to decide what was right for me. It wasn't really for me, but for all of them. As I didn't feel anything, I didn't realise I was being pressured in to having an abortion, at the time. But two weeks ago I thought I couldn't cope with a baby and have my ex-boyfriend hounding me down, his family own this town. Little did I know that, that's all they wanted me to do, have the abortion". "Why did the farther want you to have an abortion. Tell me about him". "He's married and already has a family. He bought me clothes, so I could do the modelling to pay for my uni fees". "And where do you think he got the money from to pay for your cloths", "I don't know, his dad I suppose, he has never worked, not as I know anyway". "We are talking about Jordan Butterfield", yes he got married when he was 18 his father runs the family with an ion rod". "What do you mean runs the family". "Nothing happens in the family, his father doesn't know about". "So his father wanted you to get rid of the baby"? "I don't know that, but he has a hold on both Jordan Butterfield and Dr Butterfield." "do you suspect anything about his dad?" "All I know is they own this town".

"Let's go back to the week you decided to have the abortion, oh do I really have to go over that again"? "Now but it will help you". "OK lets get it out of my system. The last thing I really remember is that we all had an argument at Jordan's dads house, and I took off and got some advice from my friend, I thought he had a level head, and he suggested going to a doctor he knew, my friend advised me to have an abortion", "what was his name again"? "jack McGregor, he said he would organise it, no question's asked".

The creative writer thought for a moment, his brain was doing over time trying to work out who every one was, and what part they played in getting this poor girl to have the abortion. He realised the three of them had got her to get rid of the baby, why? Was it too much of an embarrassment for them to accept? Colin wanted her to realise the severity of having an abortion! Although he knew, she now knows what a baby really means. As she carried on telling her story "I decided to have the abortion and now I feel stupid about the hole situation". "Your not stupid, we all make mistakes in our lives". As she started crying Colin took out a handkerchief and passed it to Jacky-May, then she wiped her cheeks and stuttered, "I, I realise know that it was all I wanted and it was a child from the moment the egg was fertilised, and I felt different from that moment on, I can't bare the thought that I have thrown away the chance of having a baby". The creative writer couldn't watch her cry, he tried to stop her from going on! As he now had tears coming down his face. "You don't have to do this at all, you don't!" Although she was crying, she wouldn't stop or couldn't stop."The baby that god gave me as a gift to cherish and nurture into a fine young thing", "Yes! A child!" She was in tears of grief, and she put her head in her hands, while wiping her face, she thought for a moment. "It was a Child from the moment I conceived". Colin stretched forward and gave her a reassuring cuddle, as the tears just flooded down her face, he wanted to help her get rid of her grief, and to let her now someone cares, when he let go of her, she just couldn't stop crying, he knew he wanted to stop her from crying, some how, so he cuddled her, until she had the courage to carry on telling her story. Colin thought to himself, I must go, this is too much to bear for me, let alone for her! Then I felt more tears coming down my face, I understood her feelings, and the situation she was in, she just kept sobbing and saying, "You don't realise, that from the moment you conceive, you have given life to a baby! Do you"? I was there for quite a wile, as she shed more tears, "god bless you. No most of the mothers that get pregnant don't realize it is a baby from that moment they made love, I am not sure I see it in the same way, because I'm a Christian. Yes I realise you are in torment". Jacky-May replied "I now believe it is a baby from that moment of being conceived. It is a gift from god, I should have embraced it shouldn't I!" "Yes you should have!" Colin reassured her, you do realize god has already forgiven you in Jesus. She looked at him with a blank face and said nothing, as if she really wasn't sure what he meant, so she asked again. "Am I already forgiven in Jesus"? " Yes you are, he died on the cross for all our sins, all you have to do is to believe in him, and ask him in to your life, she gave Colin an even blanker stare? She sat there cuddling Colin for a long time. Then she eventually started talking about her family. "My family wouldn't have let me keep it anyway, no mater what happened, so you see, I didn't think I had a choice!" Colin interrupted. "You did have another month to decide whether to keep the baby or not" then he went red with embarrassment, as he wiped his eyes. "Yes I know that I did it in a rush, I just didn't think or feel I had a choice, but to get rid of it, him, or her. What does it mater that I am a model and need to keep working to pay of my debts, my debts are the least of my worries know, I realise what life is about, and what if I can continue to go to uni, I don't really care at the moment"! "You have the choice to take it one day at a time, and I could take you to a local church for some advice on how to move forward". She sat there and thought that her baby had gone to hell because of her sine, she shouted out, save my baby God! Save my baby! Colin read from the bible don't stop any little ones coming to me, let all of the children come to me". He continued holding her tight as she screamed into his shoulder giving some comfort where comfort from God was wanted and needed. She sobbed so much, she couldn't cry any more. When she calmed down, she muttered to Colin, "What about my baby"? "your baby is in heaven with Jesus, I know your child is in heaven with Jesus and god the father. Jacky-May asked Colin to pray with her so she can ask Jesus for forgiveness and into her life. As he prayed she copied him. "Jesus please forgive me for all my sins, I ask you lord Jesus, to come into my life, and be my lord and saviour, amen. "He is always there to HELP." I have a little book of John's gospel!" This will tell you all about Jesus and if you really want to get to now him, I will arrange for you to join a bible bashing course," she laughed at Colin saying that. "Bible bashing course", she chuckled out loud. "Here have a read and I will be back later to help you, in any way I can." "okay thank you". "Do you need anything from the shops? I will be in about 11ish in the morning." "Yes please, can you get me some bonbons and a crossword puzzle book"? "would you like me to contact your family?" "Yes please here is the number of my parents, and just say although I'm in hospital, I will be home soon, to tell them what happened over here, Thank you Colin". "That is okay, I will do that as soon as I get home. See you tomorrow." "OK night". "Night!!"

PHONING THE PARENTS. He was so worried about phoning her parents, that he had totally forgotten to asked her some more questions about the doctor, who did the abortion. When he got home he looked more worried than before, so his Gran told him to go into the living room, and she will be in with some coco and biscuits. He spent all night gazing out of the window, wondering what he should say to her mum and dad, waiting for that time of night so he could phone them. He looked at the clock and thought they will just be getting up about know, and listening to it going tick tock, tick tock, tick tock, he couldn't get that sound out of his head, tick tock, tick tock, tick tock, all because he didn't want to worry them first thing in that morning, he said to himself "well its know 8 o'Clock over there, here we go!" He started dialling the number Jacky-May gave him, and the phone gave an infernal ringing, but no one picked it up. He wondered what Jacky-May would say, if he said he couldn't get through to them. You can see she loves and needs her family! Especially know, So he tried again an hour later, 9 o'clock precisely. This time it rang a couple of times and it was picked up, Colin gave a sigh of relief, but hadn't got a clue what to say. He had all that time and still didn't now what to say. He took a deep-breath! Here we go! "Hello can I speak to Jacky-May's mother please, its very important". "who is it please," "Colin Forester a friend of your daughters. Excuse me are you one of Jacky-May's brothers." "No I'm not one of the family. Call me James I'm the Butler, hold the line please". Then a strange high pitched voice came on the phone. "Hallow Mrs Braughd-Bent here! What is this about my daughter, has she got her senses back? And decided to come home to marry her betrothed!" Colin replied "excuse me are you sitting down." In a panicking voice she said, "ho no she's dead isn't she!" He could here her mother sobbing. "I knew that going to England, would be the last I would see her". "No it's not that bad, she is doing well, however she is in the local hospital, and has had an operation, and is doing well. I will try and get her to ring you herself tomorrow!" "Just tell me what the problem is- b-boy!" Colin said excuse me! "we had a storm here in ledgers town, and she collapsed over the road from me. She was taken to our local hospital." His conscience keeps telling him to tell the truth, he was sweating at the thought of telling her. Her mother was getting annoyed at the poise on the phone, and sternly said "Come on a boy! Tell me what's going on!" He eventually got the words out. "Well it appears she collapsed due to some form of bleeding and after a week in intensive care, she came around. She really wants you all to know that she is fine, and she misses you all. She will phone you as soon as she is up to it". "Is she really okay know". "Yes! She was fine when I saw her a couple of hours ago". "What hospital is she in"? "Ledgers Town Royal Institute, have you got a pen handy"? "yes! Just a minuet," {as she franticly looks for a pen} "okay I'm ready what's the number." "The number is-", "okay." "Thank you. Who are you to my daughter"? "Ho Just a friend!" "Anyway thank you, your sure she is fine" "yes!" "Goodbye sire". " god bless you". Well that went okay I think? Can I get some work done on this story know? He did a follow up piece on Jacky-May, how she rose from the ashes and is doing very well in the hospital.

THE CREATIVE NEWSPAPER

Women who nearly bleed to death in the storm, Lives due to the L.T.R.I. As he was thinking to him self while yawning, I need some sleep! The sun is rising and I want to get to the bottom of the abortionist story. Why would a doctor let anyone go home bleeding from any operation let alone an abortion? It kept worrying him as he doesn't want this to happen to anyone ells. He couldn't think of what to do about it, and what about the people it affects. The hole family looses the baby, not just the mother, they all loose out and would are on tender hooks, not knowing what to say to each other. There are plenty of victims!

As he went to go for a walk his Gran collared him, and made him have some breakfast it was a bacon, eggs, tomatoes and mushrooms. She new he hadn't slept all night and could see his mind was going haywire, the restlessness, he has never felt like this before about anyone, in his hole life. As he went out through the door he shouted "thanks for the breakfast it was what I needed. I am going to the hospital soon okay Gran I'm off." "But it's only 9 o'clock." "Yes I now I've got some things to get for Jacky-May." "Ho she has a name know", shouted Gran "are you getting on with her OK". "Yes Gran, she is a sweet thing, Do you want some shopping getting while I'm out Gran"? "Now that's OK just get yourself some eggs for the morning". "will do". While he was out, he saw the Jaguar car with one of the men coming out from the locale mortuary. He was ecstatic, this is one of the men that has been chasing me. So he works at the mortuary hay? I wonder where he is going? I know I was going to the shops, but I can't let this chance slip away. He followed the Jaguar through town and out to a country farm. As he drove passed the farm he stopped at a lay-by about a mile down the road, the lay-by was slightly hidden, it had just enough trees to hide the car although you could see the tracks of the vehicles, if you was looking for it.

Colin tried to clime the high rocky dry stone wall, it had a fence on top of it, but no chance of getting to the top, so he walks down towards the farm entrance, he watched the new born lambs. He was amazed, as he watched one of the sheep having her lamb in the field. How wonderful life is. He thought ha what would it be like to be a farmer? Having new born animals around you every spring? That would be the life. As he got to the farm yard the farmer was putting some dead lambs in the boot of the Jaguar vehicle, Colin thought OK' a cheep Sunday roast and started to walk back to his car. He was half way back to the car, when he could here the distinct roar of the Jaguar coming down the lane and it's revving engine sounded like it was racing down the lane and looked back anxiously, it was right behind him, it is trying to run him down, he was sweating with fear, so he ran as fast as he could, the car swerved in to him the first time, and he jumped as high as he could, then a second time making him jump higher on to the wall so he grabbed on to the barbed wire pulling himself out of danger. He hanged there with one foot in a hole of the wall, that saved his life. After he had finished scrambling up, he looked at his hands which were bleeding pretty badly, the barbed wire made some well and truly deep cuts in his hands although it didn't hurt. His mind was rushing and his body shaking, sweating all over with fear. I'm glad I got away with that! Thanking god he was alive he kissed the grass, he laid there feeling re-leaved he is still alive. Thinking 'What's his problem? He sat there and watched the Jaguar speeding down the lane and out of sight. That's a bit weird trying to run me down, all because I now he's bought some lamb's. What's this man got against me? Or more to the point, what do I know about him but I haven't sussed out yet! First why they Followed and chase me around town and now getting run down by him. Mind you I did follow him here! Maybe that's the problem? I must get another job this one's killing me, I will go home and do some rational thinking about what they are up to. Ho no there is blood running down my arm's and all over my nice new top, Gran will go spare! As she only got it for me couple of days ago!

But Colin cannot understand why the driver of the Jag tried running him down?, after all it is only a farm, well I think it is? I better a take a look around. So Colin jumped down and got into the car and drove back to the farm entrance, dare I go in. he thought? As Colin got out of the car and the farmer came over to introduced himself " hi I'm Mr Jonathan, Jones. J, J to my friends" {that names a bit cheesy isn't it} "Hello I'm Colin" Mr Jones said "oh … have you cut yourself?, look at the state you are in, come to the kitchen and lets wash those cuts and bandage you up. How did you cut yourself? … it's pretty bad". "It's a long story" replied Colin so we went to the kitchen and he got out a bowl, he put water and some disinfectant on it. "So how did you do this to yourself", he asked again as he put my hands in the bowl, distracting me by asking all the details about how I got the cuts, I was still in shock but managed to explain the jag that drove out of here tried running me down, his face went white as snow and he said "are you sure?" "There good customers of mine, every spring at lambing time I get a few lambs that don't make it, so he picks them up, any time of day or night. I phone him as soon as I get one struggling. He gives me top dollar for them, the same as I would get if they were two year old lambs." Colin asked "do you ask what he has been doing with the lambs". "No that's none of my business?" "He could be a butcher for all I now." "Why the extra money for fresh lambs"? "I can't work it out, but the money comes in nicely at first I thought he was freezing them as fresh as they could be but now you told me this, I am thinking there must be another reason they want them that fresh? May be that's me just being a simple farmer". "Sorry! What do you do Colin", "I work for a paper company and since I helped a woman with a saviour bleeding problem, I have been plagued by that jag and the two men following me. But today I thought I might follow them, to see what they are up to? Well I ended up here so I am at a loss why they are targeting me? Thank you for bandaging me up I must get back to see Gran 'O' yes do you know there names" "yes one that answers the phone is Cameron and the one that picks up is called Tommy" "do you know there

last names because I need some help with tracking them down"
"OK no I can't help but here's there numbers, but you will have
to do some work, as I don't know there last names". Colin had a
cup of coffee to take the edge of the shock and Jonathan said "I
should be more careful if I was you," and made some toast, that
didn't seam right somehow! But it made me feel better, and I left
there in time to go to the hospital by 2 o'clock. As I walked in
Jacky-May saw the bandages and the shock on her face, it said it
all! I just said "I will be OK in a couple of days". I couldn't tell her
what really happened today, can I? So I said "Hay has your mum
phoned yet", "no". Jacky-May was feeling low, so I read a psalm
to her as she fell asleep, I slipped away and went home to Gran
When she saw the bandages she was bad enough but when she
saw the amount of blood over my clothes, she treated me like an
invalid, she sat me at the telly, then she made me something to
eat. I felt like a king that had just come home from hunting, (He
Laughs out Loud) She tried asking what happened, but I couldn't
tell her, because I couldn't remember most of it myself, not even
where the farm is, I was stunned, I told Gran "I just wanted to go
to bed", my head was thumping "let me take a look at your hands
before you turn in", "OK Gran if you must", "it's for your own
good young-man!" Let's go to the kitchen and sort you out with
clean bandages. Gran noticed there was still rust in his cuts and
was determined to get it all out, I was wincing as she used some
strong arm, tack, ticks, and antiseptic, it was painful. "Know
then Colin you could have lost your hands with leaving that rust
in your cuts I've not seen so many bad cuts on one hand before",
when she had finished, She bandaged me up. "can I get that sleep
know Gran? I'm tiered!" "Yes love you look like you need a good
nights sleep", "yes Gran I also feel ill", "see you in the morning
love, OK son", "night Gran". "Night love don't let the bugs bite"
as she chuckled to her self.

I got up early the next morning and phoned that number's
Jonathan gave me, but it was dead. Either he gave me the wrong
number's and is in on whatever there up to, or I've put the wind
up them,

Colin went out for a walk before breakfast to get some structure to his story for the paper.

I felt starving when I came in and Gran was coming down the stares so I shouted "morning Gran did you do me some supper last night?" "yes Colin yours is in the fridge as you went to bed early" "thanks, I will have it for my lunch, Gran your wonderful!" "flattery will get you everywhere" he opened the fridge to find the biggest plate of spaghetti he had ever seen "ho yes! Its spaghetti and meatballs, Grans. meatballs are the best thing I've ever tasted, especially during a day tracing Leads. While eating his lunch he sat there thinking what can you write that's punchy, but not distasteful about Jacky-May and her situation, hmm- then he shouted "gr an I'm just going on the comp in the study" "you don't need to shout all the time. I'm old! Not deaf, and you have just got in, what have you been doing this morning" "I've just been for a walk, but I will be going to the hospital to see Jacky-May in a bit, I will be down in about an hour Gran". "Doesn't your mind ever stop son?" "No not really Gran". "Right now I need to get on with some writing. If I don't do it know I will forget what I am trying to say about the doctor." He started typing.

THE CREATIVE NEWS

YOUNG LADY FOUND BLEEDING IN MAIN STREET, LEDGERS TOWN.

The woman was a young AMERICAN student found bleeding in the high-street at the bus stop. She apparently had an abortion, and was left bleeding without any after care, from the cheep backstreet abortionists. They didn't do her any favours. As she had collapsed outside my own house and was found with severe bleeding. She was taken to the local hospital the Ledgers Town Royal Institute. I give thanks to the good doctors who work for our NHS at the London Borough Royal Infirmary she is fine. If she had gone to her local GP FIRST, she would have been better off, why do people use back street abortionists and not there local doctors? Is it because they don't ask any questions at the abortionists, or do they JUST take your money and run?? leaving you with the possibility of dying, as they are reckless and it's only the money they are after. They are a set of high class thugs. It was nip and tuck whether Jacky-May made it or not. Please I am appealing to you all, if you now anything about this doctor or doctors to speak to their Local Authority's 'Please 'Please 'Please! Tell someone!

TIME FOR ACTION. That evening he took a drive to the address on the paper, 1 the high street and found it to be right out in the open, with a back and front entrance. He saw the sign directing patients to the entrance around the back as he followed the sign through the ally way. He noticed this place is in a mess, there are yellow bags all over the place. He also noticed there appeared to be some surgical needles sticking out of some of the bags, he knew they should be in a separate container. He started looking about for the hospital policies, Aren't the yellow bags meant to be put in a furnace? So we don't cause land contamination and to keep away mice and rat infestations. This isn't looking good for a place that does abortions. I do pray this place is cleaner inside than it is out-side. He took a good long hard look at the building, and took some pictures then wrote down plenty of notes. He spoke to the homeless people that were huddled around a fire in the car park. He asked if any of them wanted any help! Not one took him up on his offer, Colin just wanted to help. He went and bought some coffee and sandwiches, so they could brave the night with a full belly, he offered some of them a warmer place to stay but none took the offer up, they are too proud to accept help, just as he was going to give up a young couple needed somewhere to stay over night. They are on there way to Smithy's town to a hostel there. He gave them some money and told them to go over the café and he will meet them after he is finished here.

There was a couple of young girls coming out as he got to the entrance, he asked them how they found out about the place, one of them said there mother told them where it was, and she got a finders fee. "A finders fee! What do you mean"? "My mum works as a nurse and any customers, she passes on to these abortionists, she gets paid for". "How does that work then"? "Well my mum passes them a business card and they then hand that in and my mum makes a bonus from the abortion clinic", "OK thank you". He thought for a moment, and mumbled "boy is this shocking, so there seams to be profit for the nurse, as she gives out a business card, she then gets a finders fee's". Her customers are by word of mouth. "and where do I find your mum"? "She goes around the estate visiting patiences. They ask her to come around to have an examination, then she will give a business card, if she thinks its OK to have an abortion". "What's the name of your mum"? Trudy? "Trudy what?" her older sister is very sarcastic and said "Come on lets go, mum will be mad if she knows we talked to someone". "Hang on what estate do you live on?!" "The Willis croft estate", "why?" "its OK no reason". He thought to himself, I must check out the legality of the place she works for.

He went over to the café to find the couple that wanted to stay over, but they were not there. He asked Trudy the café owner if she had seen them. "yes they were looking through the local paper, and said they found what they where looking for". "OK thank you".

Time to go home, I'm bushed, I need some sleep, my hands feel sore. As he got in the kitchen, Gran asked if he wanted tea but he just gave a loud yawn, "I can see your tiered tonight, go have a rest, I will make your dinner". "No that's fine Gran I had some sandwiches in town, I will go and lay down night Gran" "night son".

TIME FOR ACTION PART 2.At breakfast, Gran asked Colin"are you going back to the address on the paper"? "yes Gran its not far from here, its, 1 the High-street", as he left he shouted "bye Gran see you at lunch time" as he left instead of going to the car, he went out to the front door, Gran shouted "hay aren't you going by car" "no Gran I've decided to walk to the town centre this morning. Just because it is a beautiful day".

As he stepped out of the house he looked up at the tree's. The sun was shining through the trees, it felt like a real fresh morning, although the road was busy with traffic, you can see and here all different types of birds, thrushes, magpies and your normal pigeons, ho the swift are so fast. I do love it here. He was day dreaming while walking and looking up at the tree tops, and not thinking of where he was going, many a time he walked out in to the road while daydreaming.

The top branches of the trees looked magnificent, tremendous colours, the golden sun shining on the branches giving them a golden brown colour with a hint of green. It makes him thankful he's alive. It feels like being in the wood's. What a joy life is, enjoying nature at its best, and not thinking what he was doing, as he gets to the cross roads, it dawns on him, where am I meant to be going today? I don't want to work, I want to live. But of course he gets to the main square, and he sees the café is busy and that's a good thing he thought, I suppose I can watch number 1, The high-street from here, without being noticed at all.

When I got to The café / Coffee-house to some of you out there, with that magnificent fresh coffee smell, I felt the urge for the real coffee, it is like being in heaven, especially when they come round and give you free refills, tight you may think While I kept my eye on the abortionist's clinic. I just couldn't refuse the custard slice{just don't tell Gran}. This gave me the perfect cover on the main square. The people that came and went all seemed to be from children of about 11 years up to young adults 18. As he was watching the building, It concerned him that the building was still in such a poor state, since it hadn't been repaired from the storm, and it was being used for abortions. This is an old 1960s office block. It is made of pebble dashed prefabricated slab's of concrete, with black under painted glass to help insulation. There is glass missing and the insulation is hanging out from the corner. This type of insulation is an extreme thermal insulation material and is used as a fire wall to stop fire and smoke spreading. Although it's not fire safe with massive holes in it. This didn't look good. It's not a place you want to be at night that's for sure. He decided it was time to go in to investigate. But it troubled him why anyone would trust coming here. It smells of urine and alcohol in the alleyway. There are beer bottles, drink cans, sweet rapper's and fast food trash in the door way. It is disgusting and has a lets say chocolate smell to it, yes it smells! He looks at the graffiti on the walls, most of it was rubbish, although there was one of a mermaid that looked really cool. This is one you would defiantly take a picture of. A picture says a thousand words.

Back to the job at hand, this place needs to be condemned. Its like they don't have a clue about keeping it clean. As I went to the door that really isn't a door, it's a rusty black cast iron block, and with a guard, a big bouncy guard! The creative writer asked, with caution in his voice! "Can you help me to please"? The guard interrupted with that deep voice of his, "hay what do you want young man!" "I just want to see Doctor Rashid". "Ho no you don't! He only has women patients that have special needs, don't come here again OK", "well I now, I will arrange a meeting with him if that's OK" what special needs? He thought, then the creative writer asked "what are you talking about special needs"? "He only does urgent gynaecology operations!" and your a man! He laughed out loud at the creative writer, what an embarrassment "O I see, can you tell me what type of patients come here then?" "If that's not to rude of me" {a silly question you would think? Hey you never know unless you ask.} "all sorts of desperate women that need abortions". "Yes but what type of people? High-class, middle-class, or the poorer classes"? "It's mainly the middle class to lower class people that come here, they are all desperate to come to this practice. After all Dr. Rashid is here to help the people! That can't cope with the thought of having a child whether it be, because they where raped, or just have had an affair. First time pregnant women, that are too young to become a mother. Ho yes! There is one doctor that does transsexual procedures he's Dr Rashid's brother-in-law, they set up this practice 5 years ago and its been very successful with the amount of women and transsexuals that come through the door. I also include the pregnant children that come through here, they don't hold there innocence valuable any more" THE CREATIVE WRITER thought for a moment about the child pregnancy are they the fact of child abuse, or just nigh-eve children, they see sex on the television, thinking it must be OKAY to do or do they really think they are older than they are? Sad to think people allow there children to see sex and horror films as normal real life {no wonder we are in a mess}. Just as they where talking, a young couple was pleading for money to go to Leeds. The creative writer gave them some money and said haven't I seen you two be for, "no we just need to get to Leeds to get somewhere to live, "how much do you need then" "only another 3 quid" okay here is your 3 pound and some to get yourselves something to eat. I want to see you two over in the café in five minuets okay" "yes okay" the guard said to the couple "don't come around here again". The creative writer started talking to the bouncer about the cleanliness of the centre the bouncer said "it was in a worse condition than this before the clinic was here", I couldn't believe my ears, so I politely said "goodbye to the bouncer". As the creative writer crossed the road he couldn't see the couple anywhere this is strange another two people just vanish. I better go in and ask if they came in the café. "Excuse me" "yes Colin what can I do for you" "well I would like to know if you had a young couple come in for coffee and something to eat, they where both blondish". "Yer but I heard them say the money you gave them will get them to Smithy's town, today," "am I just a fool thinking these people really needed my help." "No Colin your just kind" "OK, that's fine, as long as they are OK", "I will see you tomorrow", "okay Colin", "goodbye Joe", "good night!"

WHO ARE YOU BORN TO BE? Back to the lets call it the medical centre, Why would somebody want to change there sex? It's none of my business, but, I defiantly want to talk to this doctor about deforming what nature gave us! I sure have enough to keep me going, my minds running away again. It is an abomination to change your sex! God made you who you are! What are you thinking or not thinking about trying to change your sex. How do you deal with this, its wrong in gods

eyes. **Children are born male or female, not ho I will be what I want to be! Transsexual operations, no thank-you. The creative writer thought that god made us to be this type of baby? And when we grow up we decide I want to be? You made us who we are Lord, and we have destroyed all you have accomplished. The story for the paper reads**

Abortionist's intentions. The abortionist, is he really thinking of what is right for the child, or is he just thinking of the money he can make, by doing as many abortions as possible. This man specialises in child abortions what is he thinking, when giving? Abortions to someone that's only a child. Has he thought about whether the whole family could cope with the baby and help out. What is his responsibility to the patient and there family, or to his profession. The question I want to ask is, does he really care? The baby's aren't born before they are to be for the slaughter. But they are still baby's at the end of the day. I don't understand these people that think it is OK to take a life that can't protect it's self.

BACK TO THE HOSPITAL AND JACKY-MAY. As he arrived at the hospital he saw the jaguar parked outside. His hart leapt in his mouth, no, no, no, not her! As he ran towards the hospital he stumbled running up the steps, he ran through the main entrance, sliding along the corridor. As he was flying along the corridors, he began to struggle with his breath, his chest was tensing up, as he was panicking that something had happened to his Jacky -May. As he got to Jacky-May's ward, he could see she was there safe and sound, she gave him a great big smile. He was so pleased to see she was safe. He staggered in to the room out of breath, Jacky-May wondered why he was running in to her ward, although she was pleased to see him anyway, and you now he was pleased to see her safe! She didn't realise, he was a nerves wreak inside. She got out of bed and stood back taking a good long hard look at him, as if there was something wrong with his appearance, he was white as snow, then she asked "why was you running in here?" As he just collapsed in the chair by her bed, he said "you really don't want to know". "Maybe I do want to know!" She was determined to get it out of him, he gave in to her demands, "okay I have been followed around town in the last week, as I was trying to find information on you, you was still in a coma. When I went into town and tried to find out, who you were and what had happened to you? I was followed by two smartly dressed men, and I had to make a run for it. then a couple of days ago, I was nearly ran down by one of them, by a farm. Then we get to today, I notice their car outside the main entrance and thought they were after you?" "Don't be silly Colin, what would they want with me", "I don't know yet but I am sure going to find out. What about your briefcase I haven't found that yet". "There was only my course work in it nothing special anyway", Colin insisted "I will watch you tonight!! If that's okay" "watch me why"? "Nothing is going to happen to me here, although I have been sort of forced into an abortion. Then all of a sudden her voice changed, in a scared voice, she said nothing is going to happen to me, it's not!" "No it's not! I wont let it!" "We must be careful that you are not left alone at any time," After Colin had calmed down, I don't think now is the time to take her around the garden? For a walk is it. Yes' Colin you do as you planed. Although he was worried! He was determined she was going to go to the garden party he had arranged. Then the nurse came straight up to Jacky-May and with a big smile on her face, asked "so how are you today my star patient". That made Jacky-May laugh and feel special, she was aware how Colin felt about her, and that made her desperate to go for that walk in the gardens with him. So she replied with a cheesy grin on her face "I'm fine let me go out please, just for today, one trip out to the gardens isn't going to hurt is it", just at that moment the nurse realised they only had Jacky-May down as her name and needed to know the full name and address, so asked for the full name, this made Jacky-May cringe, the nurse said "what's your full name" "It's Jacky-may Braughd-Bent. Can I go out then"? She was so excited to be going out of the ward with Colin, It felt like her first date, she was all bubbly inside.

Colin was still intrigued about the name Jacky-May? And

asked "why are you called Jacky-May"? "My dad had a thing about a song of a smiler name, so that's where my name came from". "I see, well the name suits you down to the ground". "You are full of compliments today Colin". Jacky-May tided herself up, and was making Shaw her hair was brushed to perfection, although make-up isn't permitted on the ward! The nurse's smuggled some in just for this occasion, this made Jacky-May suspect something was going on, {in the Meantime, Colin went to get a wheel chair} when he got back he said with a grin, come on lass get in, I will drive.

As Jacky-May got out of bed she winced as the stitches pulled, so Colin went over and pick her up and put her in the chair, then he tucked her in making sure she was well and truly covered with a white laced blanket, he had brought it in especially to make Jacky -May feel extra special. They said "Bye! See you later", "have a good time you here!" "I will" As they walked along the ward corridor entrance, Colin saw the two men go past, Colin said "Ho no not know" {and went into panic mode}. In a strange voice Jacky-May asked "what's wrong Colin", "those two men that just went past the entrance to the ward, there the one's that chased me in town the other day, and tried running me down! I must be getting to close to whatever they are up too". "There isn't any logical answer is there"? Jacky-May said "I would like to know what they have got to do with this hospital, or are they keeping an eye on you Colin", she gave him a nervous smile. Although it was meant to be a joke, she wondered what they where really up to?

Colin started humming to himself, Jacky-May new something just didn't add up, so she muttered, "Hay don't worry, we are going to have a nice walk and don't let that mind of yours runaway with its self, OK Colin". They waited a wile before checking corridor was clear.

Colin was in a hurry to get to the hospital café as quick as he could. They kept a good look out as they were walking down the corridor to the lift, Colin jumping at every squeak of the wheels, from a bed that a porter was pushing towards them. He thought

I'm meant to be enjoying this? I feel so up tight. He had mixed emotions, he is excited to be with Jacky-May but, disappointed he couldn't go after the men from the jag. I am in good company thought Colin. Jacky-May said in a stern voice, " where going out of the ward and its about relaxing and taking time out, and that means from that paper of yours to, just for one hour that's all I ask", "OK" {know who is the boss!}. As Colin and Jacky-May got to the gardens, Jacky-May saw the men jumping into there jag with some packages. Jacky-May said no you don't Colin! He just smiled and thought I will catch you up one day you just wait! And said to Jacky-May "now is the time to take you for a relaxing cup of tea". Although Colin couldn't get the men out of his head.

Chapter 4

Getting To The Hospital Café

A s they walked around the gardens and they turned around the corner, Jacky-May could see all sorts of sandwiches and cakes on the tables out side, the hospital café book store. There was a couple of nurses were there to toast Jacky-May on her miraculous recovery they all shouted, "here's to you Jacky-May". "Thank you, I don't deserve this, I'm just a patient". The nurses both said "you nearly died! So just be proud of surviving, we are proud of the way you bounced back", and the nurses had to go and attend an emergency so they said "we will be back, when we' can OK see you asap", that just left Colin and Jacky-May to talk, they chatted about there past, and there hopes for the future, Colin explained about how he was brought up by his granny, and that he still misses his mum and dad, all this time later.

THE DEATH OF HIS PARENTS. Then Colin went all serious! He explained his Mum and Dad had died in a car accident, so his Gran took him on. The accident happened when he was just becoming independent and he used this time to grow his writing skills. It made him want to be a writer for the local papers. I wanted to get to the truth of the accident. I wrote the stories for my own interest, I wanted to know why my family was wrecked by this accident, and why did the accident happen. "I just hurt!"

"oh … that's sad". "I found out it was a toy boy driver with a supped up car, that killed my parents. The car's were a complete wreck". "I see can you went through the wringer" "I was told by the police he had been on a night out". He didn't suffer any physical injury's except cut's and bruising, but as the weeks went by, I was trying to cope with my loss, and piece together what had really happened

INTERVIEW WITH THE DRIVER. "He was only 18 and when I first met him, he was a mess, he had a mass of guilt welling up inside him, and he couldn't sleep, he lost his job because he was so depressed, he couldn't go out most days. So I asked him what he thought had happened. He explained to me he wasn't drunk but had one beer, it was wet he said he wasn't speeding at the time of the accident". "So what happened to make him feel so guilty". "He started telling me that he knew, I was missing my mum and dad, but I really wasn't there to blame him, in fact I told him, I wanted to forgive him". "Why would you do that" " So I could go on with my life. Because if I blamed him! I couldn't go on with my life, I forgave him to heal myself. As I told him I forgave him, he started to cry, I said There's nothing to cry about. He just wanted forgiveness, so told him he would get his forgiveness from Jesus! That is why I said to him, I have already forgiven you! All that time he was depressed he couldn't move forwards until he was ready to be forgiven by the lord. All because he needed that reassurance he is forgiven. Then he asked Jesus into his life. After that I got to know him as a fiend, and I now it wasn't his fault, it was an accident of life. Life is what happens to some people, and they can't move on. "But you have got to forgive that person that's hurt you" "why". "So you can move on with your life". "That's why I become a news reporter, It was the effect of finding out all the facts. The truth is all I want to write. Life is hard and things happen in life, you think shouldn't happen to you and by trying to find out the truth of life. I found myself writing the local incidents in my diary, but they where just in my diary. So I decided I would look for a job, that involved my observation skills. That brought me to the local newspaper, THE CREATIVE NEWS because I found I could use words to describe what was going on in the local area", he poised for a moment and a tear ran down his cheek. Jacky-May wiped his face and said "shoo" as she put her finger on his mouth and kissed him tenderly she said "that's enough know. Let's get back to this wonderful party you have laid on". "How did you now that!" "people gossip you now".

Party for two + guests.

Turning back to the table full of food and the sight of the home made cream-cakes. She couldn't stop smiling. Although she felt sad at Colin's mum and dad's story, the party made her feel excited at what Colin had done for her, especially because of his past it really touched her deeply! {she will remember this day for the rest of her life}. It hit her in the hart, like she had never felt before, she realised then money doesn't matter, its love that matters. She looked up at Colin and some tears stared running down her face, Colin got out a handkerchief and wiped her cheek. "He said not you as well" and then whispered in her ear "this is just for you my special laddie". She said with a warm smile, "why did you do this for me" "I think I'm falling for you, but we will see who cracks first and he laughed". Jacky-May smiled and said " Look at these beautifully designed tables are they usually here, {she loved the design of things}or is it just for us", she said. "Yes they are always here. But you have some special nurses on your ward, that are astounded at the speed of your recovery, and your attitude to life". Two of the nurses arrived as they where eating the sandwiches Jacky-May asked them to join in Miranda and Katrina instantly said "yes of course that's what we came back for", as they all laughed Colin picked up his cup and invited every one to toast Jacky-May again and gave her a kiss! {on the cheek of course}. He said "regardless of what's happened to you, how we all have seen a real change in your life, may god bless you Jacky-May, hip, hip, hu ray. Hip, hip, ha ray. Hip, hip, hu ray".

There was plenty of food for all the nurses and the doctors that turned up. He then said "to all you nurse's and doctors that have helped Jacky-May back to health, I thank you all especially,

Katrina, for the cake and for the attention you gave Jacky-May, God bless you all." Colin was very attentive and asked Jacky-May what food she wanted next. She laughed at the attention she was getting, she never got this much attention, not even at home with the servants to wait on her. They had prawn cocktail's, for starters ham, cheese and pickled onion with salad it had a little olive oil drizzled over, not too much, just a hint to taste and of course, it wouldn't be right without olives and to top it of with a beautiful fresh cream cake, home made of course, cheese and biscuits to finish. All the nurses that were passing by joined In. They didn't get to learn much about each other as there was a lot going on around them. As the party wound down, Colin asked Jacky-May if she was ready to go back inside, although it was in the late summer, it was getting very chilly out there. Colin and Jacky-May said if you don't mind us going for a walk, to take in all the excitement we have had that afternoon, when Katrina asked if she could come as she had an hour to kill, before she was due back on the ward, Jacky-May said without thinking "yes of course you can", Colin gave Jacky-May a funny look, {thinking he was going to have a romantic walk} anyway while the three of them was walking, Katrina asked Colin if he had serious feelings for Jacky-May, "yes! "I like her a lot." {ho no, I sounded pompous then}, They laughed, "and when jack-May's released from hospital, what are you going to do? Colin thought what a funny thing to say, "why!" "Ho just wondering if I would get an invitation to the engagement party", Colin went bright red! "Ho okay! I hadn't thought that fare a head, but yes when it happens", she screeched, "so it is going to happen then, I'm so excited for you both". Colin's ears were ringing, the screech was so loud. He agreed it would probably happen? Jacky-May was over the moon, she didn't say a word just a big grin all over her face.

She noticed a beautiful orange and yellow rose bud and ask Colin to pick it for her? H e said "you just don't want me to get pricked by it do you". Jacky-May just smiled, he said "okay then If I must". Katrina said while your down there can you get me one to, he just laughed, what can I say to that? After giving them there roses, Colin suggested they make there way back to the ward. When they got to where they could see the lift, Jacky-May noticed the men from the corridor getting in the lift, and watched it go down to the lower ground, Jacky-May was wondering what was on the lower level? Then asked "Katrina what is on the lower ground?" "only the morgue" she asked "why! "Ho no reason I just wondered what two smartly dressed young men were doing, going down to the lower level floor, as I know there's no wards down there! Colin asked to go down and find out what they are up to, but Jacky-May and Katrina said "there's no way we are going any where near the morgue", but they suggested to Colin that they kept out of site, and watched the lift from under the trees behind the rose bushes. They could see what was going on from there quite clearly, Colin reluctantly said "okay". But he really wanted to go down and find out what was going on. But Katrina would have none of it. They argued for about 15 minuets then Colin gave in as it was 2, against 1, doesn't work. They kept well hidden and watched for 45 minuets Colin said lets go, nothing is going to happen as Colin took a couple of steps towards the hospital, the lift opened and boy did Colin jump, right behind the rose bushes, he let out a little suppressed squeal like a pig, it was all Jacky-May and Katrina could do is trying not to laugh at his noise, then Katrina saw who was coming out of the lift, and gritted her teeth, Katrina reassuringly said "Ho that's my boyfriend! The morgue assistant. He's helping the men carry the small packages to there car, before the men left they smiled with great joy, and walked back with Katrina's boyfriend, he shook there hand while they passed over an envelope, Katrina jumped forward as she wanted to run over to belt her boyfriend for being so stupid. Colin grabbed her and pulled her to the ground knowing it would be dangerous for her to run over and interrupt the meeting. He eventually he got Katrina to calm down holding his hand over her mouth, she wriggled like mad, Colin calmly told her "You mustn't tell anyone, you could be in danger! And I can only cope with one of you, being involved in this" she replied "Colin this does make me involved, so you will have to put up with that!" " please calm down Katrina". They all eventually agreed to follow the men with a focused Katrina. As they were following the men, the sky was darkening, and some how the men walked around the corner to the front entrance and slipped out of sight, before they could move in, Colin was seething underneath. Colin said "lets go back to the ward, it's the safest place at the moment!" On the way to the lift Katrina was shaking and shouting, "what has he just done Colin"? "I don't know yet, but I promise, I will find out and tell you asap". " Colin was frustrated with the situation and grumbled at Katrina" "Keep calm for at least a minuet!" Katrina said "okay, but I want to now what he's been up to!" Colin and Jacky-May said together "we don't know yet what your boyfriend was doing, but let Colin follow it up"{although Jacky-May hadn't known Colin long, she trusted his judgement}. And they took Katrina for a coffee to calm her down, when they all went back to the ward, Katrina said "I can trust you right!" "yes" said Colin "I will sort it out." Katrina reluctantly went back to her work, but was so worried she didn't want Colin and Jacky-May to leave her side {Colin was at the stage of thinking Katrina was in on it all from the beginning. His worry was about Jacky-May and replied "That girls my worry!". He pointed to Jacky-May, and they all walked in to the ward.

JACKY-MAY'S FAMILY PHONES. When they had been in the ward about 5 minuets the phone rang, it was an important phone call for Jacky-May. The nurse shouts in a sweet voice "Jacky-May, Jacky-May". There's a phone call for you, it's your family" Jacky-May shouted "Hurry darling, hurry", Colin pushed her in the wheelchair as fast as he could to the phone, Jacky-May was so nervous she kept saying, "ho I don't know what to say". As the nurse passed her the phone she said "here's the phone darling", "Ho thank you", "mum is that really you" "yes love its me" "how is every one over there"? "There fine, what is this I here you've got your self in trouble"? "Yes I was going out with a, well I thought he was someone I could trust", "Well lets not talk about that", "I am worried that you don't want to get married to your betrothed this summer, because of the man that rang to tell us how you was getting on". "Hay mum after all I've been through, and the fantastic people that are here looking after me. I would be mad to come home!" "It's that man that phoned up isn't it". "It's not quite that easy as that mum, there is a lot that I can't tell you at the moment, he looked after me when I needed it. But if he would have me as his wife, I would be mad not too. for the first time in my life I think I'm in love". "You do realise, we can't accept that! We have gone a long way getting this young man to agree to marry you, he has always loved you and you know he does, you know what it means to the family's financial situation. Both your brothers are off sorting there own lives out, but they still expect us to foot the bill, some ones got to pay for it", "It's not going to be me mum! I'm not interested in money, its love and integrity that matters to me! And you know that's not fair on me mum, you know I don't want to Marry the man of your choice, I only love him as a brother and that's all, I couldn't marry him I don't love him!" "Well you know we will have to cut off your trust fund, that you was going to get on your wedding day". "Mum I don't care about the money, it's my life, I will do with it what I please!". Jacky-May's mum slams the phone down disgusted that her daughter has let the family down. Jacky-May was so upset, so Colin just cuddled her and put her in to bed, and said "don't you worry it will all work out alright in the end."

CHASING THE EVIDENCE. Meanwhile Colin was thinking of going down to the morgue. After putting the damsel in to bed for the night. Colin asked Katrina to take him to meet her boyfriend. On the way to the morgue, Katrina wanted to make sure her boyfriend wasn't going to get into trouble. Colin couldn't promise that, so she was really reluctant to help, but out of her own disgust of what her boyfriend had done, this alone was what forced her to help Colin. Colin asked "is there any way to trace a baby's records, so I could at least have some facts to go forwards with. "Is there any D, N, A, taken from the foetus's, so they could at least track down some of the actual proof, of where each body, the foetus came from" Colin then said "I feel like this is the start of the evidence coming together to trap these body snatchers, after all that's all they are!". This is where Katrina came in to her own, she new there was a new computer system in the morgue, which had all the baby's birth names on "yes we have one of them new 'fangled' computer systems, that does D.N.A. testing in a mater of minuets", the played around with the D.N.A. computer for about 15 to 20 minuets, and Colin shouted out " There we have found the D.N.A." data base. Katrina hadn't a clue what a data base is, let alone use one. Colin went through the DNA data base and started printing out the last two weeks of foetus's that had gone through the morgue. As Colin and Katrina left the morgue and where on there way back to the ward, they got to the lift and it went on up to the ground floor, before they could press the button. Colin was desperately pressing the button, It started coming back down to the lower level, they both began to panic, there was nowhere to hide. So Colin and Katrina ran in to the morgue and hide behind the desk, they where breathing heavily, Colin trying his hardest to control his breathing, he was sweating like a pig with fright, Colin had a sneaky look around the desk to see the lift open, boy! Was it a shock to see Jacky -May coming out of the lift, Colin sighed with relief and shouted at Jacky-may, " Jacky May what are you doing. she was hobbling over to Colin and in a nervous voice said "where is Katrina, he laughed as she popped out behind him. Jacky-May gave her a dirty look and wanted to say, "what are you doing there. When the lift went up, so they all three jumped behind the desk, the first thing Jacky-May said was "sorry Katrina", Katrina said "shoos", as a doctor came out of the lift he was with someone in a blue set of overalls, but they looked out-of-place as the doctor was talking about the product his company made out of skin, you lay it on as a scare reducing agent, that becomes your own skin where its needed, and it curls up like dead skin where its not needed. After looking at some of the bodies in the coolers, they where discussing how the skin from the bodies was to be sorted out by there blood group. They went back to the lift. Colin and the two girls just wanted to get out of there, as they walked to the lift and watched the lift lights to see where it stopped. Jacky-May said to Katrina "did you know that doctor"? "No I don't think so", Jacky-May said "arr, I forgot to tell you, the matrons looking for you, so you better make your self look ill". Colin pressed the button to call the lift. As the lift came down it was dead quiet, but they could here something scurrying around like the sound of mice, but it wasn't mice they saw coming out of the broken grate, there was not just one rat coming out of the broken grate, but just too many to stay around to count. As the lift opened,the girls squealed and jumped in, Colin just smiled to himself, thinking please be quirt. When the lift stopped at the ward floor Colin took a sneakingly look out first, he sighed a big sigh of relief, as he saw the corridor was clear for them to come out. Colin said to Jacky-May and Katrina "I will see you to tomorrow, its getting late, see you at 11. o'clock tomorrow then". They all ran in there different directions, As Jacky-May and Katrina were going towards the ward, they talked about the doctor and his idea to use the skin of dead bodies, skin as a scare reducing agent, they both thought it was to spooky, and to dangerous to repeat it too anybody ells, witch they both agree not to say a thing about it. But Jacky-May couldn't keep her mind of the subject and said "could you really do that! With dead skin? "Shush" said Katrina.

As Jacky-May sneaked back to her bed the nurse that was looking after her said have you been out for a walk?, "yes it was a grand evening walk with Colin, "Colin put on a party for me this afternoon, isn't he nice I've never met anyone like him before".

COLIN ASKED ABOUT DR RASHID. Colin had been up all-night worrying about Dr Rashid and where was he? As he was walking in to the ward, Jacky-May gave him a big smile and noticed he looked a little tired, she asked "what is wrong"? Colin just sighed and said "can I take you for another walk around the garden, what after yesterday?" "yes!" As he didn't want to ask about Dr Rashid, he mumbled "Dr Rashid," she couldn't understand what he was saying, and she said "What Colin!? Speak up please!". So Colin took a deep breath, asked out right, "what doctor did you go to see at the clinic"? Before she could answer Colin said "was it Dr Rashid for the consultancy about your abortion, and was that Dr that we saw last night anything like Dr Rashid?", she calmly whispered "no that wasn't him, but when I saw Dr Rashid in the clinic he was straight with me about the abortion, and how it was meant to be carried out. Colin thought for a moment then said "he seams a dodgy character, Jacky-May whispered "But it was quick and cheep!". Colin replied angrily "Yes and you nearly died, all because of it!". With a tear in her eye she said "I just didn't want to go home pregnant."

"My family have arranged a marriage for me at home, it's with a top politician's son, Gregory Matthews," "why, does that still happen in this day and age?!" " ho yes! The family I am meant to marry in to is associated with all the top politicians in the state's, and they are arranging marriages between there families, just to make sure the old money doesn't run out. But they tend to, love to hate each other, if one opens a new hotel, the others have to do one thing bigger, causing family fallouts between them all."

"I'm tiered of that life! That's why I am here in England, to get away from the so called family, I miss them, but I don't miss the arguing, especially over who has what". Colin was very interested in her family back ground and said "So you came here hoping to get away from that hypocritical way of life!? The question I should ask is who are your family? I mean all of your family". She smiled and replied "there is my mum, dad, and three brothers, three uncles and aunts on my mums side with 10 cousins and one special uncle on my dads side, he always took us out for a special treat on Christmas eve, or when Mum and dad are at some seminar or charity ball. They think that's the way to help people in need. Colin was thinking, *its making me sick delving through her life*. Jacky may carried on "They help people that can't help themselves. But the money just gets swallowed up by the organisation, the more money that's raised, the more money that's needed". "Ha I see"

"know to my brothers, there is Brian, he's the oldest, at 26 years old, he got a degree in art and is in Paris France, he is trying his hand at selling his own paintings! He has a beautiful studio there I love to go and visit him when I can. We must go there and see him when I am better. Then there is Hugo the next eldest 25 he's in uni at Colorado doing some sort of science research, he is a bit coy about the research he does! That leaves Cliff, he is 24 and studying to become a criminal lawyer, he wants to help people, that have been convicted of a crime that he believes they didn't commit, he loves to clear there name and therefore allowing them to get on with their lives And then there's Me of course, the only girl in the family, I'm 20 learning to be a building engineer here in England." Colin was astounded at the talents her family have, and cheerfully replied "Your mum and dad must be thrilled you are all doing so well", "You would think so Wouldn't you! But what ever grade we get, Its never good enough for my Dad. My brothers are being funded by my Dad, my mum sends me some money to prove to my Dad I am better than just an upper-crust wife," "Hay you can still have your career and be a married mum!" "Dad just wants me married! And being looked after, that's why I can't fail at this". Colin just sighed. *Thinking what a family!*

WHAT SHE CALLS SUCCESS AND WHAT GOD CALLS SUCCESS IS TWO DIFFERENT THINGS. By this time they had walked all around the hospital garden, and they where ready to go back to the ward. On the way back the two men from the jag started to follow them, Colin could see the lift opening from a hundred yards away from the entrance and ran pushing Jacky-May as fast as he could, they got in the lift as the door shut, but instead of going up to the 1st floor it went down to the morgue, when the door opened it was the Dr they had seen in the morgue yesterday, not knowing what to do, Colin just held his breath in a panic, thinking what do I do, do I kick him out or just pray, sorry lord I will pray, Colin closed his eyes to pray as the Dr pushed the button to the ground floor and smiled at Jacky-May. Colin open his eyes as the lift jolted at the ground floor, Colin new the lord was in control, although *he couldn't help feeling desperate to get Jacky-May out of that hospital to a safe place.* The doctor got out on the ground floor, Colin's was pressing the first floor button franticly, he wanted to get back to the ward as fast as possible, the doctor was still in the door way, Colin said "excuse me you're holding the lift up" "yes I know I'm waiting for my two colleagues, you see I've got you now!" "who are you" "sorry that's not the point of the exercise Colin!" "how do you know my name?" " your the creative writer aren't you? You better watch what you write in that paper of yours! Or you've had it in the future, you could end up in the national papers yourself!" By this time the men from the jag had caught them up, the doctor called the two men over, as the two men got to the lift the Dr said "leave them they will behave from now on, wont you!" As he looked round and smiled at Colin and stepped one step out of the lift he turned back to Colin and said "Good day Colin! You do get the message don't you!". Colin just smiled while pressing the button franticly, and as the lift door closed one of the men tried putting his hand through the gap but the Dr said "leave him! He will wait"

As the lift starting to move Colin gave Jacky-May a cuddle of reassurance and sighed a sigh of relief. When the lift bumped to the ward floor Colin and Jacky-May couldn't get out quick enough rushing her to the ward. As the door opened Colin pushed Jacky-May like mad out of it! There was some student doctors in the way doing there rounds, Colin shouted get out of the way! They all looked on in amazement as they saw Colin pushing Jacky-May as fast as he could, the doctor were scrambling out-of-the-way, and Colin got Jacky-May to the ward in double quick time.

Jacky-May was desperate to leave the hospital, and panicking! Colin asked "if he could take Jacky-May home?" As they told the whole story to the nurses and the security guards, they searched for the so called doctor and these two illusive two men had just disappeared into thin air, Colin knew Jacky-May was safe for the moment but wanted to take her home as soon as possible. Colin asked Jacky-May to come home with him, her reply was exactly what he thought it would be. "After all that's happened here", "yes I will!".

As they where leaving Jacky-May asked Colin if she will be able to get some clothes from her home. "Yes that's cheaper than getting new ones" smiled Colin. "Your really nice, you do know that there's something diffident about you", "what even after today" "yes your not like most men Colin". He replied with another warming smile, "Well I can't give praise for that, Jesus is my guide and saviour and boy did he save us today!". As they got in to Colin's car, Colin asked about the Johns gospel book he had given her to read, "did you read the book of Johns gospel", " I started to but then I gave up, and thought this is to hard, how do I give all my problems to a god I can't see", "but the history books tell us it is all fact there are historians digging and they even found the grave of one of the most famous ring fighters its known he killed a lot of Christian in the ring"? "Yes I get that. But I read half way through it, and thought, I can't ask Jesus in to my life the way my life is, I'm a mess!" "you do realise there is a football stadium full of scriptures proving Jesus did do it all for you and me, don't you see we need him in our lives because of the mess our lives are in, you asking him in to your mess and the lord will take it and throw it in the deepest depth of the see. The extra good news is he has given you a new spirit, so your old life is dead and gone! Don't think about yesterday, you start a new life every day, from the time you wake up he is guiding us until we get to heaven". "I can see what you are saying, but it seems to easy", "but it is that easy!"

"come on lets take you to your home, to get your cloths". He took her back to her flat and they picked up the cloths she wanted, he made sure she had a cup of tea to calm her down. Then she sorted out some cloths and things she really wanted to take with her, it was a sad goodbye to the apartment she had called home for the past two years. Colin told her not to worry about this place you called home, because, Gran will be looking after her from know on, and she will be calling that home soon".

On the way out of the apartment Jacky-May noticed her ex-boyfriend walking down the road, he looked shifty as if he was expecting her to turn up, she watched him throw his cigarette on the ground and put his foot on it, a shiver went down Jacky-May's spine, as he was turning around, she said to Colin "get me out of here!". She ran to the car and couldn't have got in any quicker, even if she had tried. As he drove away from the apartment, Colin asked "what was wrong outside your place," "I saw my ex walking down the road, a good job he was going in the opposite direction". "Lets get you home to Gran, she will take care of you", "ho can't you look after me!". Colin burst out laughing, "sorry I couldn't help that, I will be there but Gran is a dab hand at knowing what people need." When they got back to grabs, Colin made sure she had every thing she needed from the flat, because he had no intention on going back there at all. Just in case today's shenanigans was to reoccur. As they parked in the garage at the back, It was getting cold and wet out there, so he took her in the side entrance to the kitchen, where it was nice and warm. Colin hadn't told anything about Jacky-May to Gran about her coming home to stay. As they walked in with her thing's. Gran got a bit overwhelmed and said "hello, welcome to the mad house love. So Colin this is why you have been disappearing all day, and all night", "yes Gran this is Jacky-May". "Come in love sit down, we will sort your room out after you have eaten. I gather you haven't eaten yet", "No we haven't eaten yet Gran". Jacky-May noticed there was a police car parked over the road from grabs house and asked, "why is there a police car opposite"? Gran said "I haven't a clue," but Colin will go over and find out what they are doing here, wont you dear? Yes Gran I will, when he came back Colin said "don't worry we are being well looked after the manger at hospital phoned the police, and they thought we needed looking after tonight, because of the people chasing us down in the hospital, we will be well looked after, she hadn't a clue he had her picture put all over the county in every police station. Colin said just thank the lord, come on take a deep breath and say thank you lord. She looked at him strange, but took a step of faith and took that well needed deep breath "here we go!". With a chuckle to herself, " thank you lord for looking after me", "Yes you did it, Weldon!". But he could see Jacky-May wasn't her self, so he asked "what's wrong, but Jacky-May had gone in her own secluded world, then Gran said "what's up chuck!". She started crying and shaking violently, screaming and shouting, so Gran went over and held her tight, so tight she would feel safe. She manoeuvred them in to the living room, with a little hassle trying to console Jacky-May. Colin is taking her suite cases to the middle room, then he went back to where Gran was looking after Jacky-may, Colin took over and Gran went to the kitchen to cook them some dinner, although she was in the middle of baking for church, Colin came out to talk to Gran about how long Jacky-May was going to stay! But she just said "shoos", I expect she will sleep for a while". At the time of a disaster Gran always cracked a joke and Colin was on the end of this one, when she said "Colin I didn't know you got married today"? Then she smiled at him, he was gob smacked at the insinuation. Then Gran asked Colin if he wanted some dinner as she was making Jacky-May some egg and chips. "do you want some" knowing Colin"? "yes that's fine Gran". After a rest Jacky-May walked into the kitchen, Gran said "how are you feeling now love."

You do realise he doesn't stop talking about you, and your situation. "He really cares, you know", "yes I now, that's why I'm here and not at my flat. We got away from there as soon as we could, just in case we got followed. While I was in hospital today some spooky things went off, so Colin suggested coming here as a safe place for me. I agree I'm safer here, I nearly broke down when I got to my place, and I couldn't stay there, it had become my home". She started crying, and shouted, "**Jesus I need you in my life!!!**" she fell to her knees, face to the carpet crying here eyes out for the feeling of loss was upon her, and asked him into her life in front of Gran! Gran said "that's good for the sole, come on let it all out, Colin take her to the living room and help her. Colin was already cuddling her, So he took her right in to the living room and put her on the couch and tucked her in with one of grabs crocheted blankets, Gran came in and sat next to Jacky-May and said Jesus can conker all our fears. Gran started praying and as they prayed Jacky-May felt uplifted and peaceful. She realised she had to forgive the doctor, and not hold a grudge against him, for what he had done to her.

The first thing she wanted to do was go and preach to Doctor Rashid! It felt like a weight had been lifted of her shoulders and piece in her hart as well as her mind. It was really urgent to her, that she phoned and arranged to meet the doctor to tell him he is forgiven for what he put her through.

Jacky-May jumped up and ran up the stares to start to put her things in the dressing table draws she felt settled in, and sorted out her things in what she called her room. That evening Colin showed her how to do a report for the paper. They stayed home for a couple of days while Jacky-May had well and truly settled in.

THE GUARD BECOMES A CHRISTIAN

Colin and Jacky-May decided to brave the place she most feared, no1 the main high street. At the front of the abortionist surgery. Jacky-May was so worried, she walked over to the coffee house for some courage and turned her back to the building. She sighed "Coffee always makes me feel better at times like this" and ran towards the café. Colin said he was going over to the clinic entrance, just to sight it out, but Jacky-may had taken so long and Colin started to think she wasn't coming over, he was thinking of ways to get in on his own, then Jacky-May tapped him on the shoulder. He jumped so high it made Jacky-may laughed hysterically, even to tears! Colin couldn't do anything but laugh at the way Jacky-May was reacting, it made him happy to see her laugh. They finely calmed down. Colin wiped her tears of laughter away and decided that they both would go in as a couple as a cover storey. They went up to the main door of the centre and asked the guard where to go and make an appointment. Colin said "we want one as soon as possible please" he looked them up and down and said "don't I know you? You look familiar", Colin replied "a good sole always recognises another good sole" that made the guard feel really good and said to him self "boy do I feel good! I've not felt this good for ages" Colin continued to talk to him, and started to find out who he is, and what he does when he's not at work? He replied "Not a lot, my marriage broke down this year, and I just don't know what to do!" Colin calmly said "There is someone that can help you, his name is Jesus the saviour of the world. "Don't talk to me about Jesus! I can't handle all this goody, goody, too shoes stuff, I just struggle with living my life as it is". "You don't have to just cope with it on your own, you can give all your worries to Jesus.

The lord Jesus Christ the living saviour, will make good out of bad situations in your life." "do you think I'm stupid, not even Jesus can sort it out" Colin said you wont know until you try"? "Copy me!". Colin recited "Lord Jesus come into my life and forgive me for my iniquity. And I forgive anyone there iniquities AGAINST ME! I take you as my lord and saviour. Amen " At that exact moment he had finished saying the prayer, his wife was praying in a church, Lord I forgive him for cheating on me, and I will help him to keep contact with his child when its born, If that's what the mother wants, he can bring him here or for her to come in to this home as one of the family, I am know ready to give up to you all these things, because they are destroying me! I'm Bottling it up lord, take it and through it away from me! "So I can't remember it any more" At that moment she felt a peace come over her and went to phone him to ask him if he would like to make this marriage work, when his phone rang he saw it was his wife and shouted out "it's her!".

With an anguished smile he said "what do I do know help me" "just answer it, it will be all right." "Hello darling I've missed you"he thought to himself, boy have I missed this woman she's everything to me! Boy my harts on fire, he eventually answers his wife " I've missed you to" they both said "can we try again"? At exactly the same moment, "it's a miracle" said his wife. They were both ecstatic that there prayers have been answered straight away. And he went home to his family, for the first time in a year, she had done a massive meal, while eating and talking about his other child, they agreed to integrate them in to the family, as soon as possible, and they also decided to go to the locale BAPTIST CHURCH, his wife asked Jesus into her life and they looked around for a church they knew god wanted them to go to. It is a little baptist church just around the corner.

KENNY HELPS COLIN GET THE PROOF OF UNDER-AGE ABORTION'S

In the mean time, Kenny the guard started to help Colin, he sneaked him in after the doctor's had gone home. Colin and

Jacky-May tried to sort through a mass of messy paper work in the filling cabinets, as he went through the junk files, he found one that shone out, a 14 year old girl, that came to the abortionist and had an abortion within a week of seeing a doctor, without her family knowing. He was devastated to find, that a doctor could give a 14 year old an abortion. And without a family planing meeting. He took copies of 8 cases so far, the patients were children of 14 or less. Colin wrote the addresses down to contact the family's. As Colin made a copy of each folder he needed, Kenny started shouting to them to hurry up, and said "the other security guard will be here soon!". As the minuets started ticking away, he began sweating about the three of them getting caught with there hands on the files. Colin and Jacky-may were tidying up and Colin jumped at a sound outside, and whispered to Jacky-may "come on, we can't get caught know, can we"? Colin kept passing Jacky-May the folders, praying she would put them back in the right order. They ran out towards the car, just as the replacement security guard arrived to take over, Kenny shouted at the security guard "what are you doing coming late, you know I need to take my wife out to night", Kenny distracted him from Colin and Jacky-May leaving as there car went past the replacement security guard Kenny started shouting louder "it's my wife's birthday, and this had to be the day you arrive late to work late". The other security guard was telling him "to calm down chill out!" Kenny shouted back "if I was any more child out I would be asleep", and said " I'm of to take my wife out, not to chill out, good night!". The other security guard just said what ever! It all seamed to work, and Kenny was well pleased with his acting mad seen. He got into his car with a real cheesy grin on his face and said to him self, I enjoyed that man! As he put the music on as loud as he could, he drove home grinning from ear to ear.

Gran saw Colin drive in to the garage, and she put the kettle on, knowing they always wanted a cup of tea. Colin gave Jacky-may a big big hug and said thank you to her, he apologized to her that they hadn't done much all evening, but go through the surgery, with a fine tooth comb, she understood more than he could know. Jacky-May's regret of having the abortion. They walked in the back door and Gran instantly said "sit!" "Here is a cup of tea, and I gather you two are starving", "yes Gran we are both hungry!". They said it at the same time and laughed at each other, Colin had noticed they did that quite often since they met and they both said "jinks", they both carried on laughing out loud. Gran said "you two are happy, did we have a good night out", "Yes" Gran, they both said.

Gran wanted to know what all that paper work is, Colin blushed and said "just some work stuff Gran. We are going on a trip tomorrow Gran, so we need to get up early, and want to have a pick nick, is there anything in the fridge you can put in a hamper for tomorrow, while Colin and Jacky-May put all the information we need together". As Colin was finishing off Jacky-May thought she would phone some of the numbers, but didn't get an answer and said "Colin there not in!! I will phone first thing in the morning is that okay"? "yes" he replied, but as Jacky-May suspected most of the phone numbers were not real, they just kept ringing or went dead. I pray the addresses are real she said. It was just then She realised Colin would have to contact these people as a Christian, and not as a reporter. She noticed it was getting late at night and Colin wanted to get an early start in the morning, She said to Colin "shall we go to bed it's nearly 11 o'clock", "hay yes darling we need to get some rest, they cuddled each other and Colin said I'm not shore where we are going tomorrow? Do you mind if we start about 8,30ish, we will get to one of them about 10,30 to 11.o'clock is that OK"? "Then we can have a pick nick if Gran's got some pick nick stuff sorted out". Colin said talking about Gran what is she doing? Gran!" "What are you doing" Gran replied "It's OK I've got it know"{Gran has got the real pick nick basket down from the spear room} Jacky-May started to ask how far they were going Colin's quick reply was, " its not far, they are all in the 50 miles away from LEDGERS town."

CHAPTER 5

HOW CAN WE HELP THE CHILDREN'S FAMILY'S

Jacky-May's hands went all clammy at the thought of the abortion she had!!! She thought, how could you take a daughter that was only14 years old to the doctors, to decide whether she should have an abortion. Could she or would she consider putting the baby up for adoption. She started to well up inside, thinking, I should have done that, as she continued to think about her own aborted child. Colin noticed her crying and gave her a cuddle, and said "are you going to be alright tomorrow, its going to get tough, helping others that have been in your situation, she couldn't say anything, so he held her tight. She asked Colin "if she would always feel like this, he replied "no you will get through it, but you wont forget it, because it is a part of you," "it feels like there's a hole in my hart, is it always going to be there, or would it go away after, I have another baby". Colin couldn't give her the answer she was looking for, all he could say "is it will get easier, the more you help others with the same problem." This is from his hart, as it was the accident of his mum and dad, that made him become a strong Christian reporter, doing his best to get to the truth about and why his mum and dad died. He is always looking for the truth, and knowing he is giving the truth about an incident to the public in the CREATIVE NEWS, this is what's keeping him going. Colin said "lets go to bed as he held her hand

73

as they walked up the stairs to bed. He took her to her bedroom landing and said "we better get some sleep." He couldn't let go, although they were outside Jacky -May's room. Colin gave her a kiss and said "I want to come in, but I can't". They held hands standing on the landing not wanting to let go of each other, Colin said good night, as Colin watched Jacky-May go in her room, he felt really sad, but he just kept staring at the bedroom door as she closed it slowly. She just got on to the bed and curled up in to a ball, she was crying the night out Colin couldn't sleep he just saw the moment Jacky-May was closing the door, over and over again, he remembered seeing her tears reflecting on her cheek. He got up to go to her room while walking slowly down her landing, not knowing what to expect, he tapped on the door, and waited for an answer, he could here her crying, so he took a look around the door she looked up at him and jumped up in to his arms, she was cuddling him as she cried herself to sleep. Once she was asleep, Colin put her in bed and tucked her in. He was opening the door to leave when it made that awful creaking sound, he stood still and opened the door slower. although he wanted to stay, he kept walking down the corridor to his room, trying not to wake Gran up, but Gran looked out of her room and whispered is she asleep know, "yes Gran she is". "Night then son", "night Gran see you at breakfast."

As the sun rose up, Colin was having a coffee on the back step, watching the golden orange sun rising, it made him feel alive, he said to himself, this is the life sitting here watching that sun rising, with my two girls asleep up stares. I will go and wake them up in a mo then there is a tap on the window, it was Jacky-May, she was shining like a bright flower with the sun reflecting on her face, Colin noticed how radiant she is, he mouthed "are you okay then". She opened the window and "shouted yes I'm fine, put the kettle on will you"? "okay will do," he got up to put the kettle on, when he heard the sound of sizzling bacon, it was Gran cooking breakfast,as he went in he said "hi Gran you sneaked down quietly, did you sleep well", "yes son". As he put the kettle on, Gran said "how about a bacon,egg and mushroom sandwich", "yes that's fine Gran", "and for the girl too" "yes please!! Came from the corridor. "Are you feeling better this morning" asked Gran "yes I think so". While Gran was cooking, Colin got the garden table ready for three hungry people, Gran shouted "here you are" and Jacky-May grabbed the first plate to pass to Colin, Gran said again "here! Jacky-May grabbed it as fast as she could and ran to the garden table with such excitement that Gran and Colin hadn't seen before, Colin said "hey you do look happy today", "that's because I've never been so happy". Colin was very surprised, but he liked the way she was looking this morning. Positively exciting, Gran sat next to Jacky-May, she had brought out the brown source, Colin's favourite, he instantly said "thanks Gran, I do love you! And I'm not the only one either, am I" "no, Gran your the best" said Jacky-May and Colin started laughing.

Gran asked "what's the plan for today", "well! Where off to try and help some people, to help get there lives back onto track Gran" Gran asked "what's the pick nick for then"? "well if it goes wrong we have something to eat and try again at the next one", Gran frowned and thought, I don't know what he has in store for the day, but well, god bless him. "OK you two, your pick nick is in the kitchen", Jacky-May thought it would be good for the three of them to go on the pick nick, and said to Gran "aren't you coming to Gran", "Oh no I'm to old to be travelling around the country, anyway I will be in the way," "no you wont Gran, your extremely good with people, especially the ones that need there lives sorting out!" "Look at me, you did okay with me, didn't you"? "Yes son but that was a long time ago, and I'm not getting any younger," "I don't wont you younger Gran, your fine as you are," "any way I only packed enough food for you two to have a good day out son," "if your sure Gran, we could do with you and your gift you have with people." "This is your journey into life not mine son, anyway I've got your washing and ironing to do," Colin laughed "thanks Gran, you are special!" "Off with you two, its time you hit the road," "Bye Gran see you tonight". Gran tided up the garden table as they went to go on there journey, in to the unknown, hopefully it will change someone's life. As they got into the car Jacky-May asked "where they were going to" "to a farm called COL BROOK FARM Smiddles lane. Up on in the hills of BRACKNELL DALE. Colin asked Jacky-May to get the map out and find the farm, she laughed and said "haven't you got a sat-nav"? "no darling, just look at the map for me please," "okay", "look up BRACKNELL DALE", "OK got it! Take the A1 out of town, Colin laughed I haven't got that far yet, were on SNODGRASS RD, take the next right to Camden Rd follow it to the A1, "okay, got you". Colin new it wasn't going to be plane sailing, but the sun was out and the sky's were blue and Jacky-May was humming to a song on the radio, Colin laughed to himself then said "I do that when I'm nerves," yes I noticed the other day in the corridor," "yes you could call it that," "well I'm just happy," Colin replied "that good, it makes me calm, and it makes you happy." "Hay what CDs have you got in here asked Jacky-May, as she looked through the CDs and found some rhythm and blues to put on. Colin felt so warm inside, while smiling at Jacky-May he replied "hay I haven't herd that for ages" Colin was in his element with a descent girl and some good music. When he got on the A1 he asked "where do we turn off " "the A42819." "OK got that".

Jacky-May asked "what are we going to say when we get there?" "I've got some old questionnaires about the abortions systems bill, and whether it needs updating or not, we can use them". "You already had this sussed out didn't you," "I try to do some things in advance, but we are lucky this time, these questions are from a year ago". Colin asked "How do you feel about, well you Know, talking about your abortion?!" "OK, if I can help someone ells, it will be for a reason I can accept". "Let's stop and have that pick nick know darling, then we can go through all the questions, if that's okay with you", "yes, I'm getting hungry know to", "okay then only another 10 miles, and a pick nick we will have! Colin couldn't have picked a better day or a better town to have the pick-nick in, as they pulled over Jacky-May said "should we have this know or after, we haven't talked to the parents of this young 14 year old Samantha Carter yet! Maybe we are jumping the gun she said", "Ho yes I see!" Colin just realise how this was affecting Jacky-May, "I'm sorry Jacky I didn't realise", she replied " it's Jacky-may if you please!" that told him, who's boss know then Colin! So Colin replied "we will grab a can of drink and get going if that's okay", "okay thank you, you don't mind do you", "No I don't mind", "I just need to get this first one over and done with and most of all, if I can help someone with my own experiences, I will" "okay, lets do it then! What's that address we have to find, COL-BROOK FARM, BRACKNELL DALE. Colin was surprised they were nearly already there! And excitingly said "its only another 5 miles to go". Jacky-May started directing" take the next turn off and follow it round to the right", "OK got that". At the end turn right then round to the right again". Colin thought this is to many right turns surely but she was right! A signpost to the COL BROOK FARM was right round the corner. As Colin turned in to the farm yard he asked Jacky-May if she was ready? All she could say was "fine! The farm was huge, Colin hadn't seen a tractor the size of a barn before and he was looking at all the man things in the yard. Wow! look at this combine harvester its as big". "Yes Colin I get it! Shall we?". "Ho yes darling we better go to the door" {it was a grand house with a door of the size only seen in films}. "Come on Colin! "Yes I'm coming". As Colin walked towards the door a young lady came out. Saying "Yes what can I do for you? Are you lost or something? The village is that way! "No I'm not lost, can we talk to you about a campaign against child abortions", "Are there really children having abortions knower days?" "Ho yes, there are unfortunately! We have a questionnaire on child abortions to ask you if you don't mind, is that okay" "No its not convenient, go away! Colin regrettably thought they had blown the only chance they had, and replied "sorry to here that!" Colin and Jacky-May was shocked and started walking back to the car, then the sound of a young teenage girl shouting "Mum!! Mum!! what do they want?" "Its okay, you go in darling, its nothing to do with you"? But mum I heard the man talking about child abortions, can I fill out there questionnaire with you?" "Why would you want to do that?" Well I want to for myself! Mum you have to let me!

Can I?" "No because if my daughter got pregnant? The baby would be brought up here at the farm, it's a great place to bring up children, a home we are proud of, so where not interested at all". The daughter ran at her mum and shouted "I need to" "well I don't want you to okay"? Colin thought what a turn around, not what I expected I looked at Jacky-May's face, it said it all. "Okay, we will go" said Colin, he is plying the long game "No you mustn't, mum! Tell them to stay"? "okay then, just for you pet! Although I don't now why?" As they continued to sort out the questionnaire, the girl said "mum aren't you going to make them a cup of tea?" "O yes, do you want a cup of tea?" "Yes please black 2 sugars and white 1 sugar please". "What's your names?" asked Colin "I'm Katrina and this is Sam", "That's Jacky-May sat on the steps and I'm Colin". Jacky-May started asking Sam the questions, and Katrina thought my daughters doing well, little did she realise what was to be uncovered? "Ho aren't you clever darling, she's a year a head of all the rest in her school, sorry for going on, I'm so proud of her". At that moment Sam started crying? as it hit her! What she had done. She tried so hard to fight back the tears, but she couldn't stop herself. "What's wrong my darling" "mum I did something silly the other month"? "what is it? I'm Shaw its not that bad!"? "But mum you don't know what I've done"? She sobbed on her mums shoulders, her mum's never seen her in this state before. Colin and Jacky-May asked if they can help? "No, I'm sure she has just over done it with her school work"? Sam pulled her self together and piped up, "mum I need to tell you something"? "Your worrying me know what is it?" "Mum listening! I need to tell yo-yo something? I had an abortion a month ago!" Katrina was so stunned she felt faint! She held her daughter tight, but didn't think she heard her right "what did you say?!" "mu- -um I didn't mean it to happen. You know me and Steve, we've been going out for about 2'years, well we decided that we wanted each other to be our first and only! So we did it! We only did it the once!" Her mum just looked at her not believing what she had herd? "And to think my little girl! she's only 14, and I didn't realize, well, she isn't little any more! "What was you thinking of, going off somewhere to do that! Well, I don't know!" Her mum looked shocked and drained, she just held on tight to her daughter Sam.

Colin asked "can we help? By making you a cup of tea or something" "Yes please! She said in a high squeaky voice. "OK where's the kitchen," said Colin, "through there on the left", "OK got it". Colin fumbled in the cupboards to find the teabags. The kettle was a brass one on the solid wood burning stove, so it was already hot, he couldn't believe his luck, he felt honoured to be helping, Katrina and Sam. Colin said "what a great kitchen!" Jacky-May sat next to Sam's mum and said "I know its a shock' and I know how she feels! Because I went through an abortion myself. I thought it was the only thing I could do? It was Just the other month, and I'm just starting to get over it," Sam,s mum just shouted "how can you know how I'm feeling?! you haven't a clue what I'm thinking, she's only a child,"? "and your a young women!" Jacky-May held her piece for a while. Then said "Yes I do, I know you think its different, but I am only 20'years old and have a university degree to concentrate on," " She thought to herself, that didn't sound right, and said "But I know I did the wrong thing, by having an abortion! I can help you two through this, if you will let me, I feel sick every time I think of my abortion!" Sam was starring in to space, while Jacky-May went on to say, "God gave me a child from the moment I conceived, there was a baby there inside me, that's the only difference between us"?. Katrina said "I'm sorry you are suffering to, how long ago did you have", she was interrupted, "a month ago", "ho the same as me!"said Sam, Jacky-may sympathetically replied "I know how you feel", and the three of them hugged each other tight. As the three of them cuddled Katrina said "we will get through this together, okay." "okay your on. Katrina suggested a walk around the farm, to help them relax, Jacky-May jumped at the chance, although she didn't seem that interested when Colin was talking about how wonderful it looked. The first thing they had Jacky-May to do was to put on some dungaree overalls and wellies. As they went on there trek. Colin started laughing as

Jacky-May was learning to clime over a sty. They looked like they where having fun. Colin was pleased it worked out so well, he decided to follow them. Colin got the camera out of the car and took pictures of Jacky-May in the dungarees, she didn't mind she had found two new friends, somebody that knows how she feels about the abortion. Colin wondered around the farm to take pictures of the wild flowers, flowers he had never seen before, he didn't feel left out any more, as the others just jelled together, it is wonderful, he thought. He was just enjoying the countryside, the fresh air and a beautiful sunny day. Jacky-May started to explain? "I'm hurting because I threw the chance of having a baby away, like it was a piece of garbage, but it wasn't, it was my child! All because of fear! Fear that people will look and stare!" Tears started coming down her face, Sam walked over to her and cuddled her, "I know that's how I feel. I threw away the chance to bring up my child, and to make a difference to the world, by being a responsible parent, I think about it every minuet of every day! What it would have become." Jacky-May cuddled her with the sympathy, that only the people that have been through it could do. Jacky-May was cuddling her with some sympathy, but this was real empathy and trickles of tears kept running down her cheeks! Because she knows what its all about. When Colin caught up with them he couldn't see what had gone on but felt the need to say nothing. Then Colin grabbed hold of Jacky-May as reassurance that it would be okay. While he held her he said to Sam's mum "its going to be alright". Sam's mum just wiped her tears from her cheeks and said in a stern motherly voice, "Shall we have that tea know then?" "Yes lets have tea". When they got back to the house Jacky-May told them about Colin's pick nick in the car, they all said "so, shall we have the pick nick with the tea then?" As Colin was getting the pick nick out, Katrina went over to help and grabbed the blanket, she directed him over to the hay field and laid the blanket down, just as if they had pick nicks here all the time, "perfect!" she said. They all sat down and Colin asked "if he could say a thanks giving prayer"? "Yes!" Katrina screeched "lets pray"said Colin,"can I do it" Sam pleaded "yes please do," encouraged Katrina. "Thank you lord for these lovely people and good food amen", "That's wonderful, thank you, lets eat. Boy did Gran put a good pick, nick, together said Colin. They all had there fill of the food Gran provided,

Colin couldn't pass up the chance to pass on a copy of the Johns gospel to Katrina and Sam. Jacky-May said at least you know now! And I will be here to support you if you want it." We would be honoured, if you can help us through this sad time. Here' my number for when I need to talk to you on my own" said Katrina. If that's OK, that's why I'm here said Jacky-May. Sam asked if she could also contact Jacky-May herself, "well can I mum! "Yes that's fine if you don't mind". Of course I don't mind". They packed up the pick nick, and Sam went to put the kettle on. As they strolled in, Sam had made some more tea, they all sat. Colin started to pray. Lord in this one room are 2 devastated young women,thank you lord for guiding us all, to get us to where we can help each other amen. This book of John,s gospel of Jesus. Please read it when you feel down, it will help you. When you are ready to ask Jesus into your lives, you will notice a big change in the way you feel about all normal day to day things. Just in the last month, I have seen Jesus help one family get back together and lead them in a life of righteousness. And this young lady next to you, I am grateful to know her, Jesus has helped her through this. If you want to come to church to meat other people god has changed, please give me a ring. Jesus will be there when you ask for his help. Here is my card, Please contact me with anything you need help with, anything! Especially just to talk out all of your frustrations. Katrina asked Colin and Jacky-May to stay a while, "Please stay a while I wouldn't have known my daughter was going through this travesty on her own, had it not been for you two, she should never have had to cope on her own. But I'm quite strong in my way's, I expect to-much of Sam, if I wasn't so strict maybe she would have come to me" Colin replies "but you wouldn't have had the chance to here a message of the lord", Katrina shouted "hey! Don't make it about god! Its my daughter I am concerned about!" This out burst shocked Colin "Yes I know that, and so does god, that's why he puts people around us, who can help," Colin tried to say it sympathetically, but the words wouldn't come out properly, he carried on "your mental scars are raw and very, very, saw for Sam."I only want you to know that you are not alone in this, we will be there. And Jesus will help you through your pain" and when you are ready to forgive and to be forgiven. "to be forgiven whatever for?" "Jesus is there to save you" "What do you mean? Said Sam. "Well you will be feeling guilty and angry that you can't forget what you decided to-do" "yes my minds been in turmoil, and I cant sleep properly" said Sam. Then Katrina asked "do you want something ells to eat?". I want to know more about Jesus iv,e been struggling with things for a while, I knew there was something wrong with our lives, but not sure what"? she got up and cooked sausage beans and chips. Katrina said"Come on lets sit at the table", know we've got guests here". They all sat down and Katrina thought it would be a great idea for Colin to say grace! Sam said "that's the second time " yes Katrina said "well this is a special day, I am going to ask Jesus into our life's. Colin said grace and after dinner he asked Katrina and Sam to say a quick prayer Colin asked them to copy him "dear lord Jesus Chris please forgive us for all our sins and I forgive all others for there sins against me and take you lord Jesus into my life to guide me in all I do, amen", "Well-done! "you are know official followers of Christ", "I feel at total peace about this, thank you for coming" said Sam "I have been trying to find a way of coping with life, but know the lords in control, and I can get on with my life knowing, I am forgiven, by the one and only true God. Katrina asked them to come back on a regular bases, so they all could have some more quality time with each other, know there is a bond there. Colin and Jacky-May stayed all knight. Katrina isn't so enthusiastic, but has realised that she is more peaceful, a peacefulness, she has never felt before, in her life.

Colin and Jacky-May went back home. It was six in the morning when they got home. Colin shouts the usual "hi Gran is there any breakfast" "yes give me a minute, will your bacon mushrooms and egg sandwich do?" "Yes that's great, we had a wonderful time and lots of fun over at COL BROOK FARM, BRACKNELL DALE how did it go yesterday. Gran it was great thanks for the pick nick yesterday. We now have good, good, friends over in COL BROOK FARM,BRACKNELL DALE now", "we do get on well" said Jacky-May. Gran said "what have you done to our Colin, he's not so grumpy ". "I really like helping him help people who really need it. He really does make a difference to other people", Dr Rashid did the abortions to this young lady also". Gran pipes up, "your falling for him then" "well I feel sort of spaced out when I think of him"said Jacky-May. Jacky-May realises Gran doesn't know what Colin is up to, helping people with there problems, so they can deal with there lives? And changes the subject, "can I have Your bacon egg and mushroom sandwich please Gran". "I'm glad he brought you home. We can look after you properly when you want a rest there's a couch in the living room, or you can go lay in your room, use it as your home. Your lucky Colin really likes you". Colin whispered in her ear "are you coming to the office, we can get some work done on the paper". Gran I've got some work to do on the computer". "Yes that's fine son". Ah Grans. actually waking up properly, she's usually a bit cranky when she's half asleep! Jacky-May decided to lay down and fell asleep in Grans. chair, Gran just felt sorry for Jacky-May and prayed lord you can help her get through this in Jesus name amen! She put her hand on her head and patted it, as she was leaving the room.

Colin had got onto the paper web site to put in a front page spread about the abortionist in Ledgers town where under age children are patients at a abortion clinic. With out there parents knowing or even having a say, on what happens to the baby, that is an inconvenience. Colin was getting really mad at this time in-case of the threats to him and Jacky-May. He could only put in the facts of what was done to the patients, and there ages,and the pictures of the practice, "done". Sleep time he looked in on Jacky-May where she was and crept over to the couch and slept, till late in the afternoon. Jacky-May woke him up flipping through the channels on the telly, when she found the Christian TV channel. She listened to the band playing. Colin said "leave this on, its spirit field," "what do you mean spirit field" said Jacky-May. "When you listen to it, it fills you up with spiritual power, you can tell that the lord is in the people, that sing and write the songs. There's more to following Christ, then most people think, it's a life style", said Colin. "Are you ready for a day tracking down this 12 year old today," asked Jacky-May, Colin was shocked "your really going for it aren't you" "yes I am, and if you think I can help with explaining to the family what I and there daughter are going through I will carry on doing it", "come on then, let get to Bradley road". Jacky-May couldn't wait to get in the car, as soon as she was in she put on a Christian CD, and started jigging about. Colin can not believe, this is the same lady he brought home from the hospital. "We are going to Bradley road can you", "yes I've already got the map and turn left after going straight through town. On to the bypass then get of at the 4th junction. 3rd exit a mile down the road.

When they got there Jacky-May couldn't stop her self from knocking on the door. Knock,knock,knock, "hello what can I do for you" {Colin was stunned to see an old lady} Colin replied "well we are doing a survey, of what people think about young girls having abortions". "Ho my dear it's terrible what some people will do with there bodies knower days, so they don't have to bring up their own children, Isn't it all wrong, I can remember a time when we looked after our children properly. we didn't have much money but boy was we happy!" "Come in my dearies what can I get you to drink" "2 teas please" replied Colin. "You wouldn't know this but I've got my great-granddaughter living with me, she's a darling to have around, she is much easier than her mother was at that age? She is always pleased to help anyone". What do you want to ask me I've only got half an hour and I've got to meet her at the bus-stop!" Colin explains "we are here about a girl that kneads some help, she is very young and Well she-e-e, he stuttered and just couldn't get out what he wanted to say! Jacky-May takes over, "We help teenagers that have had an abortion. We have a mission to help as many girls as possible! "We wanted to come to help and especial now we know you are looking after your granddaughter, we can't do anything without you saying its okay to talk to her", the old lady "gasped,"O my dearies,not my Nelly! Tears started trickling down her face, "what has she done? Colin explains that all they knew was that she had been to an abortion clinic. we believe she had an appointment to have an abortion, we pray she didn't" "What did you say?" The old lady went all flushed, her ears started to ring with the sound of the word, abortion! "Ho no what has she done to her body? It's all wrong getting pregnant then dumping the remains of a child down the toilet, it makes me feel sick, just to think of it" said the old lady". Colin passed her his handkerchief and helped her to calm down. He wiped the sweat from her forehead and waited till she had calmed down, then he passed the papers across to her, that they had on the young girl. "well we believe she has had! Colin started to stutter! An abortion, but I pray we are wrong! And that she hasn't had one. Colin explains, "You wouldn't have noticed, children are very good at putting on a brave face"? "is this her birth details?" He handed her another piece of paper "yes that's hers "what can I do if I don't know" the old laddie started crying "sorry I can't control my self god help me, what's happening to my family"? "That's OK that's what we are here for, to try and support you in your time of need", "we are both Christians and Jacky had an abortion experience at the same abortionist clinic", "she inspires me to carry on helping people that think its easy to get rid of a baby,"? "well its a bit rough where the abortionist is. Not that, that's the issue, the issue is that he doesn't seem to care about his patients, he acts like a back street doctor, that doesn't think about the consequences of his actions. And although he does have a doctorate we have found out he is giving under-age children abortions and not having them supervised properly afterwards".

Jacky-May she collapsed out side my house because of this doctor and that's how we met! She started helping me, since she has came out of hospital, and with the help a friend, we got some records of the under aged children, who really shouldn't have had a abortion at all? but we can only be here for you!"

Jacky-May explained she was going to university and found herself in this situation where she didn't know what to do, or where to go for help and advice? My family are in AMERICA I asked a friend what to do, he said he had a friend that worked in a abortion clinic, he already had the information wanted. I thought it was wearied that the friend I trusted in would have this information, but it turns out his ex girlfriend used it. I went to this doctor because the friend of mine said he was quick and cheep! You wont know that it,s being done he said, I trusted him, well I did and I suffered severe bleeding. And if it wasn't for Colin I wouldn't be here know! He's my hero!" It made the old lady feel romance was in the air. The way Jacky-May said them words. Then she thought about her granddaughter with the trauma of having an abortion, she went hot and dizzy, the stress I'm feeling just being her Gran, I feel sick this all went through her mind body and sole. She kept thinking about the love she has for her granddaughter. The love, anguish and worry about her granddaughter, stressing over keeping the secret of the abortion! "We must be going to the bus stop" I can't Waite to see if she's okay"? "Are you sure you are okay". "Yes" "then lets go! said Colin. "We will come with you only if you want us to come" suggested Colin. "yes I need a bit of support from you and god! If you don't mind, especially now! It was raining out, as they walked the old lady to the bus-stop and waited for the bus, it was late "ho my! She's never late" the granny was so worried, she got hot flushes and started to collapse. Colin grabbed her just in time, ho thank you young man, I don't know what's come over me," Colin got a handkerchief out of his top pocket and patted dry the old ladies forehead, he helped her up and sat her on the garden wall. Jacky-May cuddled her, as you would a friend. She looked so frail, the old lady quietly cried her hart out! And said "I could have had a Great-Grandchild she shouted!! Jacky-May didn't know what to do or say to help her? "My granddaughter"? She muttered "what can I say to her to make it better"? Jacky-May said "nothing at the moment, we will help you through this with your granddaughter," Jacky-May started reciting some of the bible. John-15 "these things I command you. That you love one another, the world will hate you, as it hated me, before it hated you. If you were of the world, the world would love his own, but because ye are not of the world, but I have chosen you out of the world. The world hateth you. John,14 he that love not me keep not my sayings and the world which ye hear is not mine, but the father which sent me! It reminded the old lady of her husband how he used to re-site the bible to her time and time again, it gave her so much piece she said, "it is the piece of the lord Jesus Christ that's here know, thank you God". "Yes we know it's very peaceful here in his company"said Colin. The second school bus arrived as it was pulling up. Rebecca her granddaughter could see her gram being cuddled buy Jacky-May. She rushed of the bus as fast as she could! Pushing every one out-of-the-way, and she shouted "get out of my way you idiots can't you see my Gran needs me!" They all looked stunned, one of them said "OK!!"another just said "sorry! Can we help Rebecca" she snapped "I don't know, do I. She was hurting after what's she's had lost and ran over to her Gran, thinking she was going to loose her as-well. She shouted from the door of the bus, are you OK Gran?" "Yes darling its you! we are worried about"? "But Gran you've been crying" "that's nothing, I felt the piece of the lord on me while we sat here" she stuttered. Rebecca frowned "who are you anyway, I've never seen you before your not one of Gran's. friends are you"?my names Jacky-May and this is Colin." "Are you Mormons or Jehovah witnesses said Rebecca" "no, its OK where just Christians", "or we like to think our selves as the followers of Christ," said Colin. "What are you coming back to my house for?" "We are going to help you with any of your problems". Jacky-May asked Colin "to look at Rebecca, she looks ill. It looks like you have a temperature boy is your head hot" Colin asked if she felt ill"? "I don't feel to good" "well it looks like we have the two of you to look after". At that moment she was vomiting sick. Gran said "Ho dear come on lets get you home, so you can get some of my special soup inside you". The rain was beginning to start bouncing down! "We got here just in time" said Rebecca. Gran fumbled with the key she really wasn't in a good way. Then Colin offered to opened the door, as he opened it, falling in trying to getting out-of-the-way of the rain. They all had fallen over each other. Rebecca started laughing at the sight of this theatre calamity, Colin's on his knees, and Jacky-May fell head overalls hills and Gran tripped over Colin's legs. Rebecca watching in hysterics, she tried very hard at composing herself, when she eventually composed herself, although she felt ill, she asked if she could help them up and directed them into the living room and said "I will make us a drink!" she couldn't stop chuckling to herself, this divert her mind from the abortion for just a freak moment. Why wont it go away she said! Jacky-May over heard her talking to her self and went to find out what was wrong. She saw Rebecca holding her head and put her hands over her ears she kept saying stop! stop! I can't take it, even the kettle boiling was to much, just the sound of that bubbling, was making her head pound, she tried to keep going by asking "what drinks do you want" "ow. Just make a pot of tea 'dearie'. Don't forget to bring in a bowl of sugar and a jug of milk? please my sweet" she looked in the room as Jacky-May was on her way to see what she could do for her. Rebecca replied, you always call me that Gran" she said with an embarrassing giggle in her voice! She walked in with a stumble in her walk., Jacky-May still trying to help, but it was as if Rebecca couldn't or didn't want to be helped. She saw Gran crying and asked what,s up said Gran "nothing I'm fine! she was carrying an old silver tray full of biscuits, Gran piped up "where,s the tea""sorry I got distracted." "You've been like this for ages! Oh my, its the abortion you've had? Sorry I didn't know, sit down! oh I love you!!!" said Gran Gran was Cuddling here like she could never let go. Jacky-May asked if she could help? "I saw you grabbing your head and covering your ears, what was wrong?" "nothing its gone know" "yes but you and I know it will come back, if you don't get some rest", Colin went to make the tea, he seamed to do that quit often, when people needed it. Jacky-May started talking to Rebecca about her experience, I got the voices in my head, someone was talking to me, then it kept replaying, over and over again". "How?" "It kept telling me to let go. They needed to go?

Colin had given Rebecca a book saying, "it's this one here, read it when you feel like this, it will give you piece". "And how?" said Rebecca "it's a book of the bible and Jesus will give you piece", Colin helped her read it, and although it is hard when you start reading it gets easier. Maggie-May pipes up, "it's because Colin is a Christian, and he gave me peace". Ho I didn't tell you Colin saved my life, by getting me to hospital while I was bleeding very badly. Sorry! I will start at the beginning. I collapsed in the tornado we just had, and Colin noticed me collapsing. Colin picked me up and carried me over the road to his home. Then the ambulance got me to hospital. He kept visiting me and with Colin's help and guidance, I got better. I kept reading this book it always helped. Keep it with you at all times. There was a time I got in despairer and it got that bad that I couldn't function. I got on my hands and knees in Colin's kitchen, and begged gods forgiveness and asked Jesus into my life, and boy did he give me piece. I'm not just forgiven but a princes of God. I suggest you read john's gospel, and that tells you, not just who Jesus is, but every thing you can be in Christ. The life we live is free from sin, but not just that, you will want to be just like Jesus."one thing I noticed in it was that Jesus was denied by his own disciples. And he forgave them. That was just the start of his forgiveness of the world"? "I haven't heard so much bible since my hubby died 7 years ago, just before your mum died, Rebecca! It's like it was yesterday" "its time we went". Jacky-May asked Gran if she would be okay, She looked over to Rebecca to see if she was okay too, she nodded, she would be fine. Thank you said Rebecca's Gran Colin said "here is my card give me a ring, if you want to go to church, we will pick you up god bless you". Gran said "Yes that would be nice. See you Sunday.

CHAPTER 6

MORE FACT FINDING

Colin said "On the way home "we will be going past the abortionist clinic, can" and Jacky-May interrupted him "Don't remind me Colin! It makes me cringe every time I go past this place," Colin was hoping to pop in and try to get a story from the doctor, asking why he thinks it's okay for people to have abortions? Especially 11+ aged children? They should have been protected! before they got in the situation of becoming pregnant!" Jacky-May sighed, "we can go there if you want? We do need to try and help more children, and there families to cope with the consequence's of an abortion! **I feel like an activist!** How can we stop this thing going on?" Colin answered, "By doing what we are doing". Jacky-May said "Isn't it strange how just one thing can change the course of your life"? "Yes we would never have met if you hadn't collapsed out side my house, Colin suddenly remembered the briefcase and tenderly said "did you have a briefcase with you before you collapsed?" "yes it had all my paperwork in it for my collage course work, that's all Colin". "Only it wasn't there when you collapsed", "it's no loss I can redo the work for collage again". What was your assignment about" "ho only the power station in a town called prince vile" "did you have any plans of the power station in there" " yes of cause I had compiled a complete set of plans I even gathered some of the builders records, material suppliers and the constructors that was used" "can you get that stuff together again, If I needed you to"?

"yes of cause I can its easy" " OK we can look at that later, but where going past the clinic", "don't you want to see the Doctor," " yes and hopefully, if you don't mind, I would also like to see the security guard. He was there when the clinic was started? and I want to find out what it is covering up"? "Okay quick! Lets stop here!" "I need to go and get a paper first". "Don't you get it free, working for the paper"? "Yes, but that's at home, I need one now! To see whether Dr Rashid's threat's to sue the paper has made them pull my stories!" "OK, keep your hair on!" "Sorry, there's a lot going on and I don't understand the parents allowing there child to have an abortion, it makes me feel sick. What are they thinking. Why don't they just teach them some self respect?" Colin noticed the Jaguar and said "Hey that's the Jag parked over there." "where!", "we are going to find out what is going on!" "Where not going to get in trouble are we?" "I don't know yet this feels strange"? Colin got excited! "lets see if we can find out who they are this time! Are you up for that?" Jacky-May sarcastic said "Yes I got you out of the morgue? Didn't I". "There must be a reason they didn't want me to find out about what happened during your operation". "lets go in", "okay". As they walked towards the entrance Colin had noticed they had cleaned the place up and said with surprise " Hay they've cleaned this plaice up, look newly painted walls, new carpet not one bit of graffiti on the walls, a shame the one of the 'mermaid' it was pretty good". Look at this a new reception area". The receptionist said "Good evening can I help you?" "Yes please, can we get an appointment with Dr Rashid?"replied Colin, "Yes what day do you want". "Er, what have you got for today", "nothing today, but I can put you in on Tuesday". "Tuesday,"? "yes we have a 10,15 appointment,"? "ere okay, that's okay, we will take it"? The assistant gave him and Jacky-May a card with there appointment on. She gave them a card each, "ho thank you". Colin's mind was going hay wire!! he felt excited yet scared at the same time, he wondered whether the reporting of this place actually made a difference and wondered what had happened to the security guard and without thinking he blurted out! Where is the security guard?" she replied with a sweet smile, "he left the same week he got back with his wife", "a shame I fancied him to". " Colin asked could you give me his phone number please I have some work for him and I've lost my phone today"? "yes here it is", "thank you". Colin thought for a second, then said "you shouldn't go after other peoples husbands, you should be ashamed of yourself!!". "A good looking girl like you could get yourself a fine man"{Colin was thinking as a Christian}. She looked at him and gave a sarcastic laugh, as if she doesn't care who she picks up! Colin thought for a Mo then prayed! "lord can you put piece over this place so people feel your love amen" the whole plaice went so quiet you could here a pin drop! That's better he thought. And said Excuse me could you tell me who owns the jag outside?" "no I don't know who they are, but they are in the back over there", she pointed through the doors at the back of the room. "In There, they are two big men, you can't miss them"? Colin always caries a small camera just in case of this type of situations he guided Jacky to sit down and slowly walked through the back door's, boy it's cold in this hallway, he thought. He could here somebody arguing over there insurance money. He says to himself what does that mean? I could only speculate at this moment in time. Looking through the crack of the doors at the end of the corridor, Colin could see three men in the room, the two men from the jag and well I think! He must be Rashid, surly as that's who the articles in the paper are suggesting is behind this plaice? One of the men was holding the third man. lets call him Rashid? Whether it is or isn't it that's what's troubling me. Is this the Doctor or a manager? It is getting really heated in there. One of the men was holding Rashid and the other man hit him, hit him, and then kicked him in the ribs while he had fallen to the floor, they gave him a good beating, the swollen black eye and a busted lip,you could see his ribs was hurting him and said "come up with the goods or ells you will get both barrel's, what does both barrels mean? It was a badly busted lip it was hanging, it needs stitches maybe surgery. The man just sat down holding his lip, he was pretty angry, you could see it in his eyes, but did nothing? I took some more snap-shot's of the three of them parting in bad company, but I thought! What are the goods? Then I saw the to men, come back in to the room and they went into an industrial freezer while the third, just sat watching them take what they wanted, they carried out two bags of blood and a dozen bags of what looked like three month old foetus? Ho boy I thought, I had to chance it and take some more shots, I followed them to the side door. I instantly new I needed a way to follow them, a way that was quick, there's got to be a taxi rank outside. I ran through the door to the corridor, as I ran through it, it went bang and the men jumped and turned around, they saw me running through in to the waiting area.

As he slowed down to a walking pace in the waiting area, he stared straight at Jacky-May, in such a way she new there was trouble coming. He mouthed at her don't follow me, and he went to see what's going on outside. He went out into the car park. He could see theme drive off as fast as they could. {If only there had been a police car going past just then?} Colin slipped back inside and sat next to Jacky-May, Colin was in the middle of sorting out how to find out who the two men are working for? when they were called up to go in to see a doctor, it was a shock Jacky-May was called out, go to room 2 please, Colin new he wasn't meant to see the infamous Dr Rashid today? but he was excited to be seeing a doctor today, as they walked in the door Colin was disappointed, it wasn't Dr Rashid, it was a women doctor that's blown it thought Colin. The Dr said "Jacky-May isn't it", "ere yes!" "Well then why are you here?" "I, I, I, well, we are after some" Colin piped up "where here for a check up, unfortunately Jacky-May nearly bled to death" "and who are you?" "I' just a friend, my names Colin Jason{should I have told the truth?} she smiled, It was like she was playing with us! Ah your Colin-forester aren't you? The creative writer for the Creative Newspaper? What stories are you on to at the moment? She laughed as she new what he was up to. I haven't read the rag this week" as she took a copy out of her briefcase, " Ho look at this, "UNDER AGE ABORTION" "ha" "you mean here right"? "yes! That's right" he said. The lady Dr replied with an amazing giggle, "I can let you look at my files if you want, but I can't let you into the other doctors files, feel free to use the comp to do your research. Come in, in the morning, I will see you then" "OK thank you"? It was clear to Colin, Dr Rashid was out of the picture for the moment anyway, at least that's the way it looks, while pointing to the back of the room, she said "there's another comp in the corner, behind the screen its okay, your be completely isolated, so research all you want! Colin, I love what you do!" Colin suggested "we could do with a specialist in this". She quickly replied "I'm sorry I can't involve myself, but you are welcome to use anything that's on the computer system" Colin was thinking! Anything on the system?, yes! We got you Doctor Rashid

Thank you! we need this help".

The next morning Colin and Jacky-May got there in plenty of time and took a look around the place. They looked through all the computer system and no surprises, they found no under-age patients, its frustrating, what's going on? Thought Colin, but its good being here with real coffee every 30min, but no stories as yet? Jacky-May keeps him filled up with coffee, then Colin blurts out "lets take this from a different angle, how many are 16 years old, just borderline and must have got pregnant under-age, and lets re-analyse what we have got?. Jacky-May you sort out to the age of just 16, and then getting to the ones towards the 17 mark. It took all day, she for them to sort them out and they had 150 this month just 16 years old and 129, people just 17, so they collected all the info. Colin suggested lets put together a story, Jacky-May just listens because she knows what its like to get your life in this mess!

THE CREATIVE NEWSPAPER.

16 YEAR OLD'S GETTING ABORTION'S

The younger you are when you have sex, the more likely you are to have an abortion, and that can stop you having baby's in adulthood. How can we? As a Christian nation help the parents teach there children the reasons not to have sex unless you are committed to marriage?

Once the story was written, Colin started thinking about the men in the Jag, I must find a way of getting the info on Rashid and that Jag, they are defiantly linked together but how? Jacky-May noticed he was preoccupied and asked "what's wrong"? "O just Rashid! Sorry Back to what I was doing". " Jacky-May can you sort them out by age"? The one's above 16, there should be a good reason for so-many people having abortions? is it just selfishness or circumstances, why! O why! O why? He was pulling at his hair out, knowing he couldn't do anything about it. He asked Jacky-May to sort out by area so they can go around and do some more research. "Is that OK?", "you have been my right hand, I couldn't do this without you", "yes I know, but you saved my Life, and god gave me a real purpose in life know! The things I did, I know it was totally wrong in gods eyes, but not wrong in mine. Me nearly dyeing taught me who Christ is and gave me a second chance to get a better relationship with god and Jesus, that's the most important thing to me now". Jacky-May finds some discrepancy's in the files "I've got these files sorted as you asked and found an odd one it says 19 but the information doesn't add up she's much to small"? "lets go to that one first and see if we can get some info on Dr Rashid?" Even if we don't find anything, we must keep pressing on, in what we feel the lord wants us to do!" Colin asked what the address was and said "we must go as soon as possible, to help where we can, it's in the upper "Beckingham area, yes the posh part of town!" "OK that's a great new start Jacky-May". As they walked out they saw the jag arrive, Colin desperately wanted to follow them from here, he whispered to Jacky-May "quick get in there", "what hide in here,your joking aren't you,? It's a toilet!" She said sternly. Colin went bright red "we don't have time to argue about it" they are coming this way,as Colin and jack-May scrambled into the small, toilet, "its disgusting in here!!" implied Jacky-May, "shoos I cant hear what there saying. As the men walk past, the men where talking about going to the freezer,s again, for some more packages. Colin looked out for them to come back along the corridor with the packages but Jacky-May started sneezing, "bless-you, bless-you, bless-you" whispered Colin, Jacky-May had a little laugh to her self, Colin looked displeased as the two men passed by Colin and Jacky-May slipped out behind them, walking slowly and keeping there distance, where can we get a taxi to follow them thought Colin. The doctor walked out of a consultation room with a patient "good bye". she said "hello again Colin! What are you doing know?" Colin took her to one side and told her they wanted to follow the two men, "what for?" "Sorry we've got to go now!" That's OK I'm finished lets go then" and she gave him a knowing smile,and a good hard push as if to say, hurry up then! Jacky-May wasn't impressed, and gave her a dirty look! She was thinking who does she think she is pushing Colin like that? The three of them ran down the corridor to catch up the to men, as they got to the front door the jag,was leaving the car park. The three of them ran as fast as they could to the doctors car. She was surprised "How did you know this was my car?" Colin laughed "we watch you coming in every morning". The doctor felt like a fool, but laughed it off, "come on" said Colin. He really wished he hadn't said that to Jennifer, as she put her foot to the mettle, Colin and Jacky-May flew back into there seats "wow" they said "how do you know how to drive like this?" "My husband's a rally driver." Any excuse" Said Colin " he is,he's second in the championship at the moment. Jacky-May asked "what! The British touring cars" no the world rallying championship" lets go then, I'm enjoying this" Jacky-May felt comfortable with the doctor at the wheel. The car squealed out of the car-park, the back end sliding at 90 degrees, Jennifer was looking for the Jag when she said "that's okay there at the roundabout 'by the start finish straight, Look there stuck by the road works" Jennifer started to feel excited and she put her peddle to the metal, Colin's head was being pushed against the side window, while Jennifer shouted out! I told you, we would catch them up". Colin felt a bit sick and thought, I like fast driving but all this sliding the car around corners is making me feel ill, and I cant stay sat in my seat for at least a second. Jennifer looked at Colin with a cheeky smile and said your not squeamish at fast driving are you Colin? no I'm not its just that I haven't had anything to eat this morning, any excuse will do Colin?" Jennifer laughed and howled like a wolf. Jacky-May and Jennifer got talking about Jennifer's husband, and how often she got to see him. Jacky-May really wanted to know what he was like, and what it would be like to go to a rally, at this Colin was getting a bit jealous! Jacky-May was getting all starry eyed, she thought, behave your self, he's married and you've never met him yet! "Feeling a bit jealous are you Colin" said Jennifer, "no I'm feeling queasy. As they went down the bypass keeping a good distance between them and the jag. When the jag pulled into a service station, Jennifer slowed right down to 60km, trying not to be noticed. But as they went into the service station the Jag had met up with another car, and they started transferring the packages. Jennifer drove right past them and gave a big smile at one of the men. Colin thought what is she doing we've been noticed know! As they parked up, they all decided just to get a drink, as Colin was going to get out. The man that Jennifer smiled at came over, "hello where are you going today" just out for a drive, it's a fine day, don't you think? The stranger said come on I'll get you three a drink, what would you like, Colin and Jacky-May looked at each other, as if to say what is she doing, then Colin noticed the Jag leaving. Jennifer smiled and said OK, they both thought, what is she playing at, we need to follow the jag, but we better go along with this I suppose! Coffee is OK they said. "Hay this coffee's good here, fresh ground coffee, only the best, I come quite a lot". "Ho what do you do"asked Jennifer, "I'm a courier", do you usually pick up from service station's then", yes its easy to get too for both of us so that's why. Colin and Jacky-May got out to stretch there legs and took the orders for the drinks the courier was busy talking to Jennifer. Colin wanted Jacky-May to go get the drinks, but realised it would look a bit chauvinistic, Colin didn't want to leave them two talking but had to trust everything was going to be alright, as they got the coffee Jacky-May over heard a man talking about the courier. "The men talking, where moaning that he is picking up another women! That's on her own, they where also worried about the amount of work he picks up here three times a week, with suspicious looking character's transferring parcels at all times of the day and night. Colin and Jacky-May got back with the coffee asap. Here is your coffee, have you had a good chat said Colin. "yes we have", "good, I'm glad you two are getting on so well". Do you come here often? asked Colin " "3 times a week", "ho I only wondered? While you get to now each other, we are going for a walk". "OK don't be to long! We've go to go in 5 minutes, she said like a boss does, "OK" Jacky-May said.

Colin thought who am I working for the newspaper or Jennifer? I pray she's got something to tell us when we get back. Jennifer turned back to talk to the driver as he was still babbling on about his job, Colin wanted to stay as he needed to know what the driver was saying about the package's? But Colin was determined to look after Jacky-May first. It was like the man carried on talking to Jennifer for an eternity. Colin kept as near to the car to listen to the conversation. Jacky-May said what are you doing, I'm just trying to here what he's saying, we could get a lead out of this, he scribbled in his notebook all he could here. It sounds like this Jacky-May. He said this ones twice a week it's going to the laboratory and one of the universities. I guess you get paid a lot of money for this type of pick-up replied Jennifer. This ones the saver, all I get from this, I put it into a trust fund for my girls university payments. In the next two years she wants to become a trainee doctor. He talked for what seamed like half an hour,but its only about ten mins, he just babbled on about his daughters aspiration in helping young mothers. Ironic he is carrying aborted baby's? There was only him and his daughter at home, so he makes sure he is home by the time she gets home from school. This package delivery is very important to him. He hadn't got a clue what he was carrying, contradicted, what his daughter wants to be, a doctor. And as a carrier by transporting aborted babies to the university's and the hospitals for experiments, he is missing the point of what being a Doctor really means. Jennifer said that's funny that's what I do, I'm a doctor so here's my card! Get your daughter to contact me this week (a.s.a.p.) she could get some work experience in the place I work at! Then if she's good with the patents, we can help to sponsor her to go to university. Thank you she will be thrilled,What's the catch? Just tell your daughter to contact me, we can talk about it then. The man walked away a little dazed, saying "I've got to go know, they want this package kept in ice, it will be melting soon, bye. I will see you again I hope"? He smiled knowing some time in the future. "Thanks for the coffee", "your welcome". Colin saw the man walk away from the car, so he grabbed jack-May's hand to get back to the car as soon as possible. As it was imperative they catch up the Jag, on the motor way! When Colin and Jacky-May jumped back in to the car Jennifer said that was interesting, lets see what type of laboratory it is? Come on then lets get after the jag! Keep your hair on Colin, I got you this far didn't I. We don't want to catch up the Jag, we need to follow this courier.

Colin was gritting his teeth as they let the driver leave and waited for him to get out of sight. They tailed him to near Cambridge. Then they lost him- {as he had slid up a muddy side road} -for about a minuet as they went passed the muddy side road Colin the eagle, noticed his car parked in the car park next to a small building, it looks like an old redundant industrial greenhouse. There wasn't a sign up saying anything about the building or the company that ran it? That puzzled Colin he said Let's go in and park up over there in the middle of the cars, so we wont be noticed. The courier was talking to some men in white coats, they where really pleased with there packages. The one that checked over the packages was wearing a suit, and had a cigarette in his mouth, although it wasn't lit. just for posing like a tart on the end of the streets, he was saying I'm the man, he was a real jack the lad, fooling about with the packages. The men in white coats, the scientists were not very pleased with him., Colin just about over heard them say. Just because you paid for the packages doesn't mean you own them, lets get these experiments done! As soon as possible please! You now we only have a two hour window before everything goes bad. Then he lit his cigarette and leaned against the wall of the building, looking very pleased with himself, Colin thought that's strange that a man in a suet was checking over the packages any way! wouldn't you leave it to the scientist to book them in? What a strange company. Colin took some pictures of the men handling the foetuses in broad daylight, while Colin took some pictures he wrote some notes down as usual, Jacky-May wanted to know what he had written and said cheekily hay lets look, Colin you are always scribbling in that pad of yours, Colin passed her his note book, but Jacky-May couldn't read it, she sighed and said what's this Colin, I can't read a thing you've written. Colin laughed and said sorry you can't read it. It is all written in short hand. Then Colin saw the man in the suit look at one of the bigger packages, as they were being taken in and said "hay that's worth the three thousand bucks on its own! Look at these beasties get them in to the labs as soon as possible, come on then they started arguing over who was in charge. The driver just left he wasn't interested in what he had taken there, or who was in charge, he just wanted the money, It made him. He was in and out in less than 5 minutes.

TAKING A LOOK AT THE EXPERIMENTS

The building was like a massive glass house, but with most of the windows white washed, you couldn't see in straight in the building. We went over to have a look to see what they did with the babies bodies. We could only see in through a small window that was left open. A strange smell was coming out of it. We could see the baby's on a surgeons table, It seamed like the most important bit of the babies was the cored, it was cut of all the baby's, and they cut the cord in to small bits and put it into several flask's, then added different chemicals to each one. and the foetuses cut up into smaller components. He went to the phone and made a call to a hospital but Colin couldn't here what hospital they where going to.

Jennifer started running to the car and said, Its time to see where the courier is going, come on! {this was to cover up the thought of this baby being chopped up for spear's, went right to the hart it felt wrong}, although she was a surgeon.

They ran to the car and yes! Jennifer drove like a loony to catchup with the dispatcher. not surprisingly, Colin and Jacky-May hadn't got in the car properly, Jacky-May shouted "are you trying to kill us! or are you just out of your mind", "I'm sorry I just had to go after the courier". He wasn't far away, so she slowed down to a normal speed. Colin was struggling with the madness of her actions, she wasn't acting rationally. She was erratic bordering on madness, Colin just couldn't trust her every movement. She was meant to help finding out where Dr Rashid is, and track down all the illegal movements of the men in the Jag. we still don't know who they are?

We followed the courier but he just disappeared in the traffic. We had to stay on the road to London. We struck lucky and court up with him just past Cambridge to a hospital training university that specialised in antenatal care. We parked up and talked about the hospital using what was naturally available in the locale system. Wouldn't they just use what was locally available to there university. It was strange that they didn't have enough of there own foetuses to experiment on.

Jacky-May suggested we go in and find out what they actually did with the bodies. We put together a list of questions to ask the head surgeon. Colin was pleased with this out come, and said at least we've found two users of the foetuses are.

Aborted babies are highly required, by scientist's and universities said Colin. Why did it frighten me through to the bone. We decided to put the questions together as we all had our own thought's about abortion's. Although, I don't know what the doctors would think about us asking questions on the use of aborted baby's. So we went in to the hospital anyway.

The receptionist was a young teenager, just out of school. Jacky-May asked if we could look around and see what the training hospital did, and if we could ask some questions from a doctor later. The receptionist called the head doctor down to the reception. The head doctor came down and took a liking to

Jacky-May so she was the one they were interested in, they wanted to know her view's about abortions. The doctors were so pleased to answer any questions Jacky-May had to ask them. Jacky-May is feeling all emotional about her first question. She said in a shy voice. Do you buy in aborted babies and if so why? Tears start running down her cheeks as she thought about her own abortion! Colin gave her a supporting cuddle. Then the head doctor went red and looked very uncomfortable, big beads of sweat started running down his forehead, he took out a handkerchief and wiped down his face. He took his time answering the question, but he eventually answered "yes! We use them with the trainee surgeons and doctors. We want them to determine how old the foetus is, and whether it was developing properly. Do you try out any form of resuscitation with any of the baby's to help the development of science, or to see how far you can go, to develop a baby out of the womb. Ho Yes! He was proud of this question, almost Bolshie with his answer. We want to save any baby that we can, so there are experiments to enable us to save another baby with that condition that the parents already love, but we are not quite there yet. We have brought a couple back to life but brain dead, so no successes yet. We are trying to save baby's lives here and not to abuse the aborted foetus! We are advising all the women that come here to go full-term. But that's only works in 4 out of ten women, and although we have a lot of aborted baby's. We never have enough to do all the experiments we want to do, and we have to do to find out how a baby forms in the womb, and what forms first and why it forms that way round, so we can replicate it out of the womb. We try all sots of things from saving parts for transplants, test them against our data base to see if any are compatible with a child already in the system that needed anything we have in stock. We have tried to grow the limbs, so that we can give the baby who needs a transplant, anybody parts, they require, that's part of our job. In a way of helping those people that want healthy baby's but cant conceive it properly in the womb. We must try and give that child a normal life. It is Therefore better for us to get the most out of a foetus They can save lives. We also want to save and transform a babies life if we can. we will do almost anything to do that. What about the financial cost? yes its getting expensive from time to time because of the shortage, but we can only pay the current going price,

Colin started having a thought that Jennifer was in with the selling of foetuses? But she has helped so much, I will give her the benefit of the doubt, but am I right to. They showed us around there top of the range surgical areas. As they where leaving, Colin asked if they could come back for an interview with a national paper and surprisingly they said yes! Know its time to relax and go home. Boy has it been an exciting day, but I'm very tired. Colin suggested to Jennifer to take them to his house as it was going to be late when they got back.

IS, DR JENNIFER A SPIE.

On the way home Colin quizzed Jennifer. About her job. Do you work in an abortion clinic to save the teenagers lives, or are you secretly in to foetus experiments. {Colin thought each foetus is worth a fortune so why not for her?} It didn't start out that way, I wanted to help young people to cope with life's consequences, and the disappointments of getting pregnant, while in a relationship to young. Some of the girls that come to my practice,are girls that have slept with there ideal one to be. {the Other half} just as there friends do. But that just destroyed there life's. A case in question, a girl who has been raped. That's a life we have to try and get to a place where they can cope, not just with the idea of aborting the baby, but to help sort out her life. I also help out by passing them on to the psychiatrist. And some are just hormonal women, just like the teenage boys, over sexed but we make sure they know the consequences of having sex under age. Jennifer told us of an family friend, she really liked and wanted to go to bed with. He said no several times. So she went and slept with a friend imagining that it would be the same as if it was her fantasy! She felt blessed she didn't get pregnant, thank god! Because she felt ill thinking of it know. It wasn't her lover or the one she wanted, she realised she should have waited for the one and only love, that would be provided for her.

Colin was shocked, this women they just met was driving like a touring car ace, and talking about god. What's worse, works for a abortion clinic! Life is crazy? They got to Colin's house and Gran was putting out the kitchen rubbish, she shouted "what have you been doing today. Your boss has been on the phone about a Dr Rashid. He's been trying to put an injunction on you over your story about his clinic". "Okay Gran I will get back to him with my new story."{that's very interesting I have an abortionist trying to close down my story's and I have his employee working with me? Strange,} "Gran can you make us three a cup of tea please!. Jacky-May wasn't pleased with Colin, asking his Gran to make them all tea, so she pipped up,"can't we make tea for your Gran instead, Yes! Yes! We could, if you want too. Colin and Jacky made tea for Gran and Jennifer. Jacky-May introduced Jennifer to Gran as Colin hadn't done so. "Jennifer's a doctor, would you believe it, and she has helped us with the abortion story, that Colin's writing", "nice to meet you, I will do some dinner when your out of my kitchen". "No Gran! I told me and Colin will do tea, that includes dinner OK," Gran sat back with a smile on her face. "What would you like for dinner Gran! Does everyone like stake and kidney, Yes! Yes! And Yes! Well Colin were making stake and kidney pie for dinner". You do the veg and I will make a pie, its my favourite said Jacky-May. That's fine darling, potatoes, greens, and carrots", "I don't like doing the veg said Colin", then Jacky-May got a strop on with Colin and said, "but if you don't do the veg no one will be eating", Colin groaned and knuckled down to it, all done! And what about some more tea? For Gran and Jennifer, okay! Gran what would you like to drink, with your dinner, Gran suggests a bottle of red wine. Ah know your talking said Jennifer, what wine do we have Colin? We have a Cabernet Sauvignioun 2 bottles, and 3 bottles of a nice desert wine. "The three castles, an Australian, I think, I can't read the label's properly, a very sweet wine", "okay! Ice the sweet wine! Open and let the red wine breath at room temperature." Gran said "know Jennifer! you can tell me all about your day job. Come in to the sitting room we will get some privacy there!" Colin take them in to the living room Jennifer grabbed the red win, Colin said "no its okay I will pour it out", Colin was making Shaw that its at room temperature first. Colin the visitor is waiting"? "Okay Gran," {boy is Gran in a bossy mood, my dear old Gran. Gran had noticed how close him and Jacky were getting, and thought she's got him under the thumb quick! But if she asked him, he wouldn't admit it. She had a real good chuckle to herself and Colin notice and said, "what are you up to Gran!" "Nothing dear absolutely nothing", "your telling fibs Gran, come on!","nothing at all", but kept chuckling to her self, "I know that look Gran, what are you laughing at", "nothing darling, absolutely nothing", Jennifer new exactly what Gran thought, about Colin and Jacky-May, and Jennifer agreed with Gran. The two of them just couldn't hold there emotions any more they started chuckling out loud, and Gran said "she's got you babe". Colin blushed, as Gran kept on laughing, she thought, my Colin is known of the shelf!

When Gran had calmed down, Jacky-May started laughing, and Colin just realised, he couldn't do anything but laugh at them, he was chuckling just like Gran, trying not to let it show. Then Gran reminded Colin to phone his editor. "I can't while I'm laughing like this but "okay, I will when I've calmed down. I get it Gran, the jokes on me! I will get you back for this Gran!" Colin is a bit stiff necked usually and doesn't know how to let his hair down but it seams Jacky-May is changing the way he thinks. "Gran, I better make that call to the editor", as he went in to the hall to phone the editor of the paper, Jacky-May followed behind him and pinched his bum, although a little embarrassed he turned and kissed Jacky-May on the cheek. Colin instantly said "do you want to go out for diner tomorrow". "Yes that's just what the doctor ordered". While Colin was on the phone the others set up the table for dinner, Jacky-May cheekily sipped Colin's red win and thought it was pretty flavoursome, she shouted "Colin your dinner is ready", "I will come when I can", but he kept talking on the phone for about half an hour and the others have already started the apple pie and ice cream.

Colin explained to the editor, what they had found out in the last couple of days, about the abortion clinic, and we managed to track down three of the young girls and with a little help we are getting then some counselling. Its great with an insider helping us to get to the truth about the illegal abortions and we found out that Rashid had disappeared from the abortionist clinic in fact, in to thin air, he has just completely disappeared, although we are positive we will catch him in the end to get him on trial for the abortions!

He explained to the editor there has been a lot of changes made over at the clinic, since we took up the story, and we found it challenging to find out the truth, about all the under age abortions there have been in that clinic, over the last year, I think that's all I can tell you at the moment, bye for now.

He eventually got his dinner, while the we girls where having a chill out with the wine, and a good old chin-wag. When Colin had finished his dinner, he took a good sip of the wine and told Gran "they where going up to the office". "So that we can sort some of the paper work out, for tomorrow's paper, there's so much to get through it might take all night," "call me when you are ready for a cup of coffee", "okay Gran thank-you"," Jacky-May can you help Gran brings the coffees up please," "yes of course I will, come on Gran we will sort out this washing up, then I will take up there coffees, If you must Jacky-May but you now Colin and that paper, he will be up all night if he has a chance", "yes Gran I now that something he will never stop doing".

Colin put Jennifer in the hot seat in the middle of the room, and said "know Jennifer, I'm going to ask you some serious questions, and lets start at the beginning, what's your legal status at the practice you work for?" "I am just an employee of the clinic", "Who runs the practise and why put an abortionist clinic, in the centre of town", "I assume Dr Rashid is in charge of the practice and I Havant seen him in the last month, since your paper started the story about the clinic's moral ethics. I am there as an employee and I take all legal patients during the day"? "does that mean you do illegal ones at night", "no it doesn't! And after all I helped you find out today that's the thanks I get from you! And you think I would do illegal work? "I clock off when I have finished all legal surgeries which is all I do, thanks for your confidence Colin!" "I'm a reporter that's what I do, ask question's! Especially ethical ones". "Why are you here in this run down town, Jennifer? After all your better than this, what I meant to say is, that you came from a better back ground"."It needs good surgeons to take up the slack,(extra work) in this area, I'm a good surgeon and I needed the extra cash. There's so much work here, it made sense to me at least to give me the best chance of getting a good wage, and plenty of practice on the surgeons table". "How can you abort a child for none medical reasons?" "I do some for non medical reasons because the patient is just a child!herself". "What medical reasons do you do an abortion for?" "If I save a life by aborting there baby because they have a hart condition, then that's a good reason to abort the baby isn't it"? Colin agrees "okay I hold my hands up some are necessary! That's it questioning over with now, lets get down to brass tack's. So will you help me to get to the bottom of the illegal abortion's at this practice you work at, and are you allowed to give this information to us". "Yes and Yes! I will help you all the way!'". "So Jennifer can we get into your company computer from here? And is it legal" "yes I do a lot of paper work over the internet that's easy, give me the keyboard". "Can you get up them files Jacky-May sorted out earlier?" "Yes there put in a folder called finish projects!" "what was the youngest you found on the system?" "Just 13 years old that's the one we started with, trying to sort out her name and address" "Freddie Trump. Bogners, lake farm, upper Beckingham". "The next one's a girl that's was nearly 16 years old", "and what's her name?" "Her name is Jackie Frizzing", and what's the address?", "she lives at Green, Marsh, Hill,Top Farm, Upper Beckingham, well, that is in the same area. May-be we can do 2 in one". "What would you like to do in the morning?" "I don't know ow!" "We still haven't found out why the babies? Foetus? Are sold on the open market. And not sent to a government ran incinerator? or a government run research organisation"? Dr Jennifer said "that's easy, its easy money, baby's and good bodies parts are big business to right person. Its always the highest bidder. There's a lot of money in research of the lambs and embryo's".Colin asked "who is the first one in the list is?" "she's 13 when conceived and "Colin interrupted with sarcasm, "most girls start there monthlies at 13, it makes me sad, she got her childhood taken away from her. Who is the father?" Jennifer shakes when he says it, and replied, "That does not say who the father is, and no we don't and wont ask that information, as this interferes with the patient's recovery time", "That's crazy, you wont ask that type of questions, No that's down to the police, to get that information, it's not a doctor's job", Jennifer rebelled "I concentrate on my job, and not anybody else's". Colin statistically replied "so what are you doing here then, if its not your problem"? "My reputation is on the line, I will always seek out corrupt doctors or nurses". "Yes I understand you are here to find the truth of what went wrong when Dr Rasead got away with doing some dodgy operations, and letting the patient go home unchecked." "do you now where Dr Rashid is?" "No I don't, and that's not my problem ether, but if he does dodgy abortions? Its my reputation I'm trying to keep in tact". Colin said "I will go and find Dr Rashid, and if your up for it, we will go there tomorrow?"

It's late do you want to stay in the spare bedroom, I'm tired so I'm going to bed,if you want to stay up please do. Jacky-May, are you okay darling {that really showed Jennifer how much he thinks of Jacky-May. If that is okay with both of you. And I have some new toothbrushes for you both. He laughed. Then Colin took Jacky-May to one side and apologised about not involving her in the conversation. Jacky -May just smiled and passed him a piece of paper she wasn't just sitting there all night as he thought, she was doing a sketch of him and Jennifer. Her attention to detail was brilliant, he thought this girls' brill. He really started to notice her in a way he hadn't of any girl before. Colin blushed and said that's fantastic. Are we going to have that dinner tomorrow asked

Colin to Jacky-May she politely said if you've got the time I will. Colin thought if we've got time, I will make time, he replied as I ignored you in the interview and it made me see you as a young lady, yes I want to go out with you," he took the girls to there rooms and eventually said thanks to his grab for everything. His hart was beating so fast as he past Jacky-May's room when he eventually got to bed, he couldn't sleep he laid there just thinking of her, He new he hit the jack pot with this young filly. He just stared into space all night.

The alarm went of at 6 o'clock in the morning, so he got up and started to make breakfast. Jennifer was the second one down which disappointed Colin, he wanted to make breakfast for Jacky or Jacky-May, as he thought Jacky-May he started singing. Yes I'm flying so high, I touched the sky. Well that's it then he thought. And Jennifer has been trying to attracted his attention! He was miles away on a plane I think. She gave up shouting at him, as that just didn't work, so she tried clicking her fingers in front of his eye "sorry I was" "yes! I gather she is a nice girl well young-lady," she said very sarcastic "having her own eyes on Colin". She knew there was no chance, she had to think of something good trying to attracted his attention with some sneaky tack ticks. Just as Jacky-May came down Jennifer made blatant a pass at Colin, he just stood back in an abrupt way. "No!" "Ho am I interrupting?" said Jacky-May. Colin said "yes thankfully! "Sorry Jennifer I'm not interested". She went red "that's okay,I had to try, you are an intriguing young man, and she ran to the bathroom." Jacky-May sat down and drank her tea, while Colin made them all, yes including Gran, what a miracle, a full English breakfast. As they were all finishing of there breakfast Gran said "you better get of to work all of you. I will do the washing up, thanks Gran. Gran had done them another pick nick, she said "here is a pick nick for today. Don't you three get to used to me making you a pick nick every day, this is the last". Okay thanks Gran you are the best. Colin asked "where we are going today Jacky-May, "I'm the driver today not the organiser", it's a bit of women's lib, I suppose you could would call it", "Chauvinism!" "Hay calm down it's only a joke". Colin was in an antagonistic mood, not his usual self, placid and calm. Jennifer looked at him with disgust, as he was meant to organise the next visit,. He asked Jacky-May, what,s the next one on our list, Colin I told you last night it was 5 miles from Sam's house. That's okay then we know where we are going. Jennifer really wanted to do the driving, so she jumped in the driving seat and revved the engine like a rally driver {that's not surprising then} as soon as Colin asked Jacky-May if she wanted the front seat, she said "Colin your not with it today, just get in and lets go". "Go through town down the A2 out to teddington then the A424 to Beckenham well find the sign posts to Bogners lake farm". "Okay that's easy today. "There are 2 next to each other. Well if you wouldn't know it 5 minuets to get to the A2 and just 5 mins to get to Teddington",{Yer you guest it the fastest doctor in the west}. As they got to the Teddington turn of. Colin noticed the jag going into the town centre, Jennifer didn't need telling she was after them a soon as she could get of the A2, they went round and round in circles just to get to the centre but didn't see the Jag any where, Colin started to say "let's get to the address, its a nice day, may be we can have a pick nick there, as we did the other day". "Well see Colin we haven't got there yet, and your thinking about food you've just had breakfast, the girls were not impressed as they went around town, looking for the way out, Jennifer saw the jag and started to follow it. Colin noticed Jennifer had slowed down and only then realised why, "Ha you was quick off the mark, without telling us!" Jennifer just laughed yer well I'm the one on the ball today. Colin couldn't believe what he saw, the Jag appeared to be going in the direction of the farm. Colin noticed the signpost it, and the Jag speeded up, it went flying past the farm, Jennifer wasn't going to stop at the farm ether!, as fast as the jag went Jennifer went faster. These two cars speeding down the country lane was attracting attention from the farmers. Colin really didn't like the look of this. big ditches on each side of the narrow country lanes, Colin was holding on as tight, as he could to the handle above the door. The speed of the chase was making Colin feel really sick. But Jacky-May was spurring on

Jennifer to go faster, until she noticed Colin had gone a funny colour of white {green in anybody else's book} she didn't say a word,but passed Colin a plastic bag, Jennifer started laughing, "not feeling to good again Colin, "you can't blame it on not having breakfast, can you?" "No it must be the squealing of the tyres, every time we go around a corner. And the ditches we might end up in". Jennifer didn't say another word, but slowed down, to lets say a reasonable speed, just keeping the Jag in sight as it turned into a drive to a mansion house, no sign saying what the name of the mansion house was. As they tried to drive in the gate, it closed on them they very nearly hit the gates as soon as the Jag went in past the second barrier, that was a bit to close thought Colin as Jennifer screeched to a halt, just missing them. "Well Colin what do you want to do know! You know where the jag lives"?. Jacky-May said "why don't we drive round and see if there's another entrance. So they drove along the lanes hoping that There's going to be another gate, but no not a gate in sight, but there is a broken down wall, the problem wasn't getting over the wall, it was getting through the under growth, the trees were thick and the bushes are hard to get through, but there seamed to be a path just the other side of the woods. Colin went first but turned to see if both the girls are OK, Jennifer wasn't impressed with Jacky-May's idea of finding a way in to the estate, Colin had got over his green phase. Jennifer started having a ball, she was spurring Jacky-May on, "Calm down Jennifer they might hear us coming". You could tell Colin really wanted to get to the house first, but decided to hold back for Jacky-May, she kept stopping. It took a good 25 mins to get to the mansion. Colin could see the car in the garage-block, the driver was cleaning the inside of it. That seamed a little strange to Colin. "Let's see if we can get to the house with out being seen" said Jennifer, she was in a hurry, but she had high hills on and couldn't walk without making a noise so she stayed behind, Colin and Jacky-May are determined to find out why the jag came here? They both ran as fast as they could across to the house ducking and diving under every window trying not to be seen, then they eventually got to a side door, one would call it the servants entrance. Colin tried the handle and it was locked, he could see the key in the lock, Jacky-May wanted to have a go at poking the key out of the lock, Colin stopped her just in time as someone was coming down that corridor to the locked door, they could here them talking, but couldn't here what was being said. Colin had noticed there was cleaners in the mansion house. The noise of the people in side was getting to close, they had to scamper back to the hedgerow, where Jennifer was hiding. Jennifer said to Colin, she wanted a go at getting in, Colin said I don't want you to go on your own". "aren't you a doctor!" She just went red and didn't answer, she asked to borrow Jacky-May,s shoes, Jennifer is going to ignore what Colin had said. Jacky-May swapped shoes with Jennifer and off she ran, like a whippet out of the starting gate, leaving Colin well and truly behind. Colin thought lets get out of here, but he couldn't leave Jennifer, so he decided to follow her and leave Jacky-May in the hedgerow. He asked her if she would be okay she just gave a scary sarcastic smile, and he gave her a reassuring cuddle and said "it will be okay, just stay here, don't you dare move". He had his work cut out trying to keep up with the infamous, Dr Jennifer. He never new her second name this puzzled him for a moment"? He finally caught up with her by the door he and Jacky-May was trying to get in to before. But to there surprise, it was ajar they could here some one bragging about the amount of money they made in one day, Colin and Jennifer assumed it was the men from the jag, but it wasn't, it was a cleaner, he was bragging, he had just found a ruby studded bracelet on the back seat of the car, and the owners offered him a thousand pounds just to return it. He phoned the master of the house, to find out if he could drop it off, as it happened his bosses had another trip into Ledgers town to do. Colin and Jennifer couldn't believe what they have just heard, there luck is in today. Colin looked inside the doorway, on the right was the kitchen, he could see the dinning area from the door way. It was clear, so he creped through the kitchen into the dining area with Jennifer in tow. These are fancy doors to the dinning room thought Colin,They tried the doors but the inner doors were locked Jennifer just smiled at him then she took a pin from her bra, he couldn't believe his eyes. There's this doctor feeling down her bra, but he didn't know what she had clipped on to it, she started picking the lock, it was open in 5 seconds flat. Colin was amazed at what she had just done. He followed Jennifer into the dinning room to find it wasn't a dinning room at all, it was a swanky playboys office. They could see a desk at the other end of the room partly covered with a flexible partition. Lo and behold Jennifer was picking the locks of all the draws of the desk as soon as she could, and in the last but biggest draw they found some evidence, that the men actually owned their own laboratories. Jennifer realised it wasn't going to be easy to catch these body snatchers. As they could always say they are on there way from or to there so-called laboratories with the foetus. Colin took photographs of all the evidence they could find, there is the sound of someone coming down the corridor to the kitchen Colin and Jennifer froze to the spot and started looking for somewhere to hide Colin ducked under the desk as Jennifer ran across the room and hid behind the door, the cleaner looked into the playboy office, she shouted "Kevin didn't you lock the office doors before you cleaned the kitchen", "yes I think so, why what have I done know" shouted Kevin, by this time Colin was getting cramp in his legs and Jennifer was trying her hardest not to breath, as the cleaner walked passed her and looked around the room, checking all the draws to the desk and cupboards, Colin was frozen to the spot in cramp and beginning to panic, it was a miracle he wasn't seen, as he looked out at the cleaners skirt from under the desk, he could see the cleaner clearly and was amazed she didn't see him. Jennifer tried to find somewhere ells to hide and could see, she could hide behind the couch, as the cleaner was checking all the cupboards Jennifer slowly lowered herself to the floor and sneakingly crawled along to the couch and just as she got behind it the cleaner said who is there? I can here you she walked around the room and said to herself I must be hearing things as she walked out of the office and locked the door behind her Colin and Jennifer gave out a sigh of relief, Colin got up and sat on the char, and Jennifer got out from behind the couch and just sat on the arm nether one said a word, you could hear a pin drop as they listened to the cleaner working in the kitchen she was there for what seamed like hours, before turning the kitchen lights out, Colin and Jennifer could hear the cleaner walking down to the end of the hallway. Colin said that was close lets get out of here before we do get caught, but he wanted Jennifer to open the draws of the desk again, as he thought he saw a document that might be handy in closing down the abortion clinic, she slowly walked over to him, he was getting agitated, and said "come on women hurry up!" Jennifer said "its okay, she has gone, we've got the rest off the day," Colin replied no we haven't Jacky-May's out side waiting for us, so hurry up, don't take it so seriously we will be finished in a minute as she opened the draw Colin grabbed the folder and said lets get out of here, Jennifer lock the draw then the went to the door connecting the kitchen you could say they were out of there like jack flash. They scampered back over to Jacky -May in the hedge row, but they were seen out of the windows by one of the house cleaners, not knowing they had been seen they took there time going back to the car, Jennifer asked to look at the folder and she was very impressed Colin I think you've hit the jackpot these papers will definitely close down there operation's. Colin noticed Maggie-May was straggling behind and went to give her a hand. He helped her to get through the bushes and undergrowth, as they were climbing out over the wall the police were coming up the lane behind them towards the gates. They jumped in and Jennifer put her foot down like always, the rally driver, she didn't give Colin or Jacky-May enough time to get in properly, let alone buckle up, Colin shouted watch out "where not in properly". As she drove past the front gates of the mansion and the police car coming towards them. Know Colin really wasn't surprised at her driving skills, let alone her lock picking skills, although he couldn't work out who she works for. He said "well your a dark horse". She just said "I don't know what you mean Colin! Let's get out of here, the police are right behind us" Colin couldn't understand how they managed to get down to the bypass, by the time the police had driven in the gate, to the mansion house. Colin was having a hart attack, so he thought! Him and Jacky-May just looked at each other as there wasn't much you could say, to the things this doctor could do with a needle? Let alone the way she drives the car? Colin said in a very quirt voice, "let's go to the girls farm shall we! We can't be done for helping people", what farm was that we had to get to Jacky-May?. Jennifer just said "we will be going passed the farm in a minuet and we can have something to eat there", Colin said "how can you think of food at a time like this? While I'm panicking back here". "Calm down Colin, we have an alibi! We are going to be at the farm in 2 minuets", "okay!" Replied Colin. She's even thought about our alibi, Colin's mind was going a thousand miles an hour due to Jennifer, I can't work her out, what is she?

When they drove in to the farm yard they all sighed a sigh of relief. And jumped out, to stretch there tension away. Jacky-May asked Colin to massage her neck and down her spin. Jennifer said "I could do with one of them", Colin just said "I'm all out of massage", all this tension was totally due to all the thing,s that happened at the house, Jacky-May couldn't believe her ears when Colin said about the lock picking in the mansion house? She just said "well I never! Did you really picked the locks Jennifer?" "Yes, shush, this isn't the time or the place, but if you want to know, I was taught by my uncle Trevor, he was a real crook, and got away with it most of his life. But it caught up with him in the end".

CHAPTER 7

JENNIFER'S FIRST CHRISTIAN OUTREACH

C olin said "Jennifer how are you at talking to mothers or fathers about there children's exploit's, "I am a Doctor after all", lets see then"? Jennifer said "I will go to the door, if you two get the questionnaire out of the boot"? "okay well done!" said Colin. Colin asked Jacky-May if she was "Okay". "I cant believe her driving" said Jacky-May", Colin said " I am just pleased to be in one piece, after this mornings shenanigans".

As Jennifer went up to the front door of this run down farm, house, a man came running out at them shouting, "what do you Jehovah witnesses want?" "Hay calm down and where not Jehovah witnesses, where just plane old Christians" replied Colin. "How did you know we were coming any way"? asked Jacky-May. That doesn't matter just go! I've got nothing to say to you! You hypocrites". They didn't notice that he had an axe in his hand, because of the amount of abuse he was shouting out! It was amazing in a bad way that no one got hurt. As the man's wife came out trying to calm her husband down, Colin asked "how did he know who we where". Colin tried calming him self, but the man wouldn't. He swung the axe at Colin, Colin ducked like he never ducked before. Jennifer tried calming him down but he stood there swinging the axe and shouting you pigs! get out of here. As they duct and dived they circled around him. As

116

Jacky-May's spoke to him he turned around and responded only to Jacky-May's voice. What is it people notice in her? is it that people notice in her the hurt they are going through, or has she just got the knack god blessed her with. She looked in to his eye,s and he responded by saying hay your alright are you love! She said "what's your name?". "Sidney", "okay Sidney tell me what's the mater? What has made you this mad"? He shouts at her, "that stupid women of mine!" "okay! Calm down know, you don't have to shout! Tell me everything that's got you this upset". He started shouting again saying "leave me alone". Then he sat down as if he has just tired himself out, all his energy sapped from him, he collapsed in a ball on the floor. As Jacky-May calmed him down, she really got to feel his hurt. He started crying, she put his head in her lap, he sat up and started crying on her shoulder, all his emotion was pouring out. She said in a very calming voice, "hey what are you crying for". He replied, "She went and got an abortion two months ago, doesn't she realise, I would have loved to be a grandfather". His wife Jemimer walked out saying "since he found out our girl Jemimer, had an abortion he's been totally depressed and off his head", "do you know who the father of the baby is, or am I pushing my luck at this moment in time". "No its fine, It's one of her cousins, he was 14 and she is just 13 now, but it has been very bad for us all". her mother said "I couldn't allow her to be a teenage mum. I didn't tell Sidney, until it was over and done with. As you can see he took the abortion really bad. When I told him I had taken her to the abortion clinic to get rid of the baby, it really made him crack up". He knew you was coming because he sees the future in dreams, some times his dreams are a curse, and some times they are a blessing, but I never saw him react like this, to a dream before. He is usually kind and generous, to a fault, but he has been totally depressed, I can see you can help him! as you calmed him down. I couldn't go through this again! It taught me and my daughter a good lesson, no mater what is happening, don't hold it back, tell your partner the hole truth not your truth? If he had known from the beginning? He would have supported my daughter through her pregnancy".Jennifer replied "I come from the practice you went to with your daughter". Jennifer explained! "These two friends of mine, have noticed a lot of things that don't agree with the ethical practices in such a specialised field. I want to start explaining that a doctor Rasead that has done a lot of our operations, has taken some short cuts which wasn't good enough" "get on with it! and what's it got to do with me and my daughter"? asked the mother, Jemimer' "Well Jacky-May explained your daughter is named Freddie? In the records" "No Jemimer!" "Yes we now that know, but why was your daughter put down as Freddie?" Jemimer went red and flushed "I didn't want it in her records, but I guess that's all out know". Colin interrupted "sorry can I go to the toilet?" "Yes go straight along the hallway the door on the right at the end of the hallway". "Sorry Jennifer I've got to go" said Colin. They could here Colin saying "hi Freddie" to Jemimer, "I'm not Freddie, I'm Jemimer!"? {was Colin testing what Jemimer the mother explained}

Jennifer said "Surely someone took your id? Jennifer tried to carry on, but Jemimer the mum started shouting abuse at them! "Who are you, are you with, the social services?" "Calm down!"said Jennifer. "We are here as a doctor, a writer and the third person is someone that's been through an abortion herself Jacky-May! And she knows how you feel about Jemimer's situation." "What are you really doing here shouted Jemimer! {the mother}?" "I said just know, we don't want to upset you. We are here to help your daughter cope with it better", "My daughter! You don't know my daughter!" "No! I wasn't the surgeon that advised you on what you should have done? But we all know what she is going through, we can help you and her cope, not forgetting the loss your husband feels about the baby? Surely, especially you want us to help your husband"? "Yes he needs your help, I know that. My daughter, she must have gone back to her bedroom, I will call her on her phone its better than shouting the house down, can I borrow your mobile to phone her?", "yes that's fine here" "ho it's a touch screen", "do you want me to prone her for you?" yes would you please"? "Jemimer your mother thinks it would be a good idea that you came down please"? "hello my names Jennifer I'm the Dr", "no go away I don't need anybody just go away!", "can I speak to her" "of course you can" " darling I would like you to come down and talk to these people?" "I don't want to talk to anyone!" "Come on they want to help, if I have to, I will come up and bring you down", "what's so important that I have to come down?" "for you and your father, do you want to see your farther in this state again, and because darling there here to help us, its better if you come down". A few minuets later the girl looking much older than before came down and stood in the door way. Jennifer asked "does she usually look that old and where dresses that way?" "yes I do! If that's any of your business? I chew gum as well! Is there anything I can do for you call it? Colin introduced every one to Jemimer the daughter and started to ask how she was coping with the abortion? She tried acting tough and said "I'm alright and coping well thanks". Colin said quietly "you don't have to act all tough when you know your crying inside?!" "You don't know what I'm going through, any of you people?" "no I don't! But Jacky-May does, she made the same decision you did, and wants to help you?" "So Jacky-May, why don't you tell me how I feel?!" "Angry! Ashamed! And most of all you realise you loved the child, you just got rid of," "well your nearly there, I'm ashamed I let that person near me!" "what person?"asked Jacky-May. "My wonderful cousin, they think the sun shines out of his" "yes okay we understand!"said Jacky-May. "No you don't! They expect me to get married to him? When I'm 18, I don't think! Even if he becomes a millionaire! I think they wanted the money his family has, that's why they kept it quiet, to keep up there life style?" Where going skint! As mother would say!" "No! No!! No!!! That's not true, you thought by sleeping with him, you could help solve all our family problems? But it doesn't work like that. With trust between two people who love each other. But money defiantly doesn't solve problems, it starts to create new problems. Me and your farther are sorting them out, its got nothing to do with what you do with your life! You thought, the only answer to all our problems was money? Well it's not! We still have plenty of money coming in, your dad works hard for what we have. You don't realise how lucky we are? You think that money can solve everything. didn't you"?! "Where not here about your money problems". "No! But they thought if I got pregnant they could get some out of his family. It makes me sick! But I miss the, well it was a baby? When it was in me, I don't like the way I got pregnant, but I began to love the child in me, and I felt I couldn't keep it, not for money that's obscene? And I feel completely empty and lost. My heart yearns to have the baby back, but I'm at a loss as to what to do?! All I know is it made me sick, what I did just for money its poisoning my mind and body". Jennifer replied "That's why, we are here to help! Colin and Jacky-May are Christians, I'm just a doctor! That's tagging along to see if there is any medical problems I can help with? As Jacky herself has had problems with saviour bleeding after her abortion, she knows exactly how you feel. Have you had any bleeding since the operation? As you know I am from the clinic that you went to see Dr Rashid. As it seems he wasn't as good as he made himself out to be? Jemimer started shouting and screaming at Jennifer, "I just want it to stop! This hurting and get rid of the loneliness I feel, know the baby has gone!" "Calm down and we will help you through all your pain", " do you mean you are hurting mental torture or a physical pain"? "My stomach wont stop hurting", she was screaming. It made Jennifer grab Jemimer and pull her to the floor, and asked her, "are you bleeding?" "no! It just hurts!" "pull your jumper up and I will see if there is any thing wrong?" Jennifer felt the girls stomach and explained it felt hard and swollen inside, so she called for an ambulance! Then Jennifer asked "was there any medication given to her a week or so before the operation"? "Yes but they didn't work!" "So I had to have the operation", "how long was you bleeding for after taking the tablets?" "Just a day and a half", "was it flowing or just a trickle"? "just a trickle" "It defiantly feels like you still have a swelling?" The ambulance arrived and Jemimer was so scared, she begged her mum to go in the ambulance with her? mum replied, "You didn't have to ask me! I was coming anyway"! Jemimer and her mum started on there way to the hospital, and that gave them time to sort some things out with the father. The paper head line is

ANOTHER VICTIM OF DR RASHIwD.
ABORTION PILLS THAT DIDN'T WORK,

Dr Rasead left another victim with a badly done abortion. It turned out that the another girl had an infection from the abortion Dr Rasead had done. She had to undergo an operation to repair the damage done by Dr Rasead. And there is a possibility, she was given counterfeit medication, the staff are going through there stock on the invoices to determine why this happened **Yours thankfully The creative writer**

While Jemimer was in the operating theatre. Jennifer arranged with Jemimer's mum for them to go back and talk about the abortion with an psychiatrist.

The Dr that performed the emergency operation came out and said to Jemimer the mother, "The Operation went well, all she needs is a couple of days observation and that should be it", okay then see you soon".

In the mean time Colin, Jacky-May and Jennifer went to upper Beckingham, to see the other child in the area, her name is Maggie frizzing at Green marsh hilltop farm. On the way there they went past the mansion house a shiver went down of Colin's spine. And Jacky-May said "did you feel that?" "Yes it was weird!" Colin asked "what are we going to do with all the info we have on Rasead, due to us going in there?" Jennifer wanted Colin to do a front page spread.

DR RASHID DESTROYS CHILDREN'S LIVES.

Although We didn't find out who the two men are that have helped Dr Rashid. He has damaged many young women in the last two years. He doesn't know how to finish of the operation's properly which means they end up dangerously infected in many ways, there is a young lady that was left bleeding and if it wasn't for our own creative writer she wouldn't be alive today. We know where they are held up. We will get you in the end Dr Rashid. yours thankfully_**The creative writer**

GREEN MARSH, HILLTOP FARM

Colin seamed a little out of sorts he only feels fine when things are going at 100 mph {but not when Jennifer is driving}. LoL. When they got to green marsh hilltop farm. There seamed to be a well balanced family. Getting on with the normal day to day things on the farm. As they got out of the car the farther said "hello are you lost?" "No were not lost. We have come to talk to you about this questionnaire". Colin had the questionnaire in his hand and asked "could I ask some questions we have about abortions? It's something that we are doing as a church, hopefully we will have collated enough information over the next year, to find out what people think, and what they want to do about abortion clinics". "It's milking time, do you mind coming back?" "It's okay" said Colin "we will wait if that's fine with you"? "Yes that's fine, my wife is in the kitchen, I will tap the window" as we are standing next to the kitchen window, he shouted, "darling can you make these people a cup of tea please darling?" She opened the window and said "yes that's fine darling", "hi I'm Colin this is Jacky-May and this is a Doctor friend of ours Jennifer". "I'm Stephen and my wife is Sonya and we have a daughter called Jackie. What was it you wanted us to fill out?" "Its not quite that simple we are trying to help families of people that have had abortions, and that's what our survey is about". "What has this got to do with us? We Havant had an abortion in the family ever". "Ha, in that case could you three do this survey for me? I need an outsiders point of view". "I've got the milking to do. Well you two girls can do this, its more of a woman's thing, I don't get involved in woman's things". " Colin replies "In that case can I come and watch the milking as it was always something I wanted was a farm?" "Okay you can help if your really wanted to be on a farm, as the cows line up in there stalls, you can clean there teats with this cloth, then put the suckers on there nipples". "Okay got that! As the cows came racing into the stalls, Colin started to get a sweat on, he was so nervous about cleaning the cows teats properly and setting them up for milking. As soon as he put on the sucker, it pumped out gallons of milk an hour. By the end of the milking, Colin decided he really likes being a farmer and thought, maybe I could do it when I retire?

As we walked back to the farm house, I talked to Stephen about his daughter, and if she had many boy friends and especially in the last couple of months, "yes there was one three months ago but he dropped out of sight when our lass become ill? I don't know what was wrong, but we took her to a doctors, well my wife did, I still don't know what it was. I know the last time she saw the boy friend she came home in a right state, maybe the wife knows why he dropped out of sight"? As Stephen opened the door his daughter was crying, he didn't know what to say. "what's wrong with you darling?" asked Stephen, Colin said quietly,"I gather these questions are hitting a raw nerve"? Stephens wife said "Please sit down darling, we have some thing to talk about!" She continued with "You remember Jackie's old boyfriend"? "Yes!" "Well darling we've been talking about him!" "You see, he got Jackie pregnant, then he took her to a back street abortionists". She has just told me. She isn't suffering and everything seems to be okay. Jennifer suggested we take her to the doctors tomorrow"? "ho why, if everything seems okay"? Darling we must do that, just to check? Well you never know knower days do you"? "Do you feel okay darling? You do realise, I wouldn't have minded being a granddad, but maybe there's another one to come when you settle down with a descant boyfriend? You are only young! It's just as well we know now". Stephen asked us to leave. We left as quickly as possible and on really good terms, I asked "if I could pop around to do the milking one evening? He was fine with that, so me and Stephen do the milking together once a week, and it makes me realize, one of my dreams to become a farmer for one day a week at least.

Colin went back to the abortion clinic the next morning and

was looking through the records, there was so much paper work to go through and very little of the official paper work related to Dr Rashid. It seams Dr Rashid used another name, Dr S Tony It wasn't easy for Colin to track down many more patients, where Dr Rashid was involved.

Jacky-May started back at the university, she found it a struggle to concentrate on anything other than Colin and Jennifer. The work they are doing, trying to sort out the under-age abortions, how many more would they uncover? Colin picked Jacky-May up that evening and arranged to go and have tea with Jemimer and her family, on the way there Jacky-May asked "what was going on with the case on Dr Rashid?" we {meaning me and Jennifer} have found over one hundred other cases over the last year alone! And he's been around for the last five years. "So There's a lot of work for us to do, if you want to?" Jacky-May just smiled and nodded. They got to Jemimer, and there was a wonderful gazebo outside with what looked like a hundred people there. Jacky-May and Colin just looked at each other because they couldn't believe there eyes. Jemimer her mum and father were actually smiling and you could tell they where full of joy. Colin went up to Jemimer and asked "what's changed?" she just laughed,and said "that's the new paster over there, don't you think he's dishy"? Colin blushed as usual and shrugged his shoulders, "Colin that doesn't answer the question?" Jacky-May said "no it doesn't, you will have to wait for the answer to that question." Jemimer "Come on in the tent, I've got some people for you two to meet, here is my uncle Charley, and aunt Mabel, they are fans of yours Colin, they follow all your stories in there locale paper". Jemimer left them in the lurch. Colin said "isn't she looking so much healthier"? "yes! And I believe its all up to you two,"? "No there are three of us helping to sort out peoples lives, and we must give all the credit to god! Charlie replied "yes I see what you mean, they started going to the village church, which Charlie wouldn't go anywhere near until a month ago, after you came to see Jemimer. What was it you did, that made my family get this close again?" "I cant say really, but the love of god!" "thank-you very much!" said aunty

Mabel. Colin said "they asked Jesus in to there lives. So it's not me and Jacky-May you have to thank, but god and Jesus for saving us all". "What can I do to help with the people you are tracking down" said Charlie. "Are you computer literate?" "yes! I can do some computer work for you, what do you want me to do?" "It is all computer work that needs doing, We have to go through all the clients of Dr Rashid and check all there birth certificate details against the birth and death register to find the ones that have been forged or just taken a dead person's identity", "we need to help the ones we can and my writing is important to me", but gods job is the most important of all". "Will you help me ask Jesus into my life?" Asked Charlie " yes of course I will, we will say a prayer and you will have become a Christian in the best seance of the word say"!

Lord Jesus I ask you to forgive all the sin I have done in my life, and all I have been. I forgive all that others have done to me, and I ask you to rule in my life, so I can follow in your foot steps and help to change the world amen!

The most important prayer to say in the morning is <u>THE LORDS PRAYER</u> and it goes like this. <u>**Our father who art in heaven hallowed be they name, they kingdom come they will be done on earth as it is in heaven, forgive us our trespasses as we forgive those that trespass against us, and lead us not into temptation and deliver us from evil, for thine is the kingdom the power and the glory, for ever and ever amen!**</u> "that's all you needed me to tell you, the rest is between you and god. We will guide you with bible studies if you want to"."Yes" said his wife with a warm hart and a smile!

The next morning Colin was back to work at the clinic, with a throbbing head, still sorting paperwork, LoL. Colin really enjoys himself sorting through the computer and paperwork, making sure they matched.

The two strange men the ones with the mohair coats, came in to the abortion clink, instead of going through to the freezers with there accomplice they asked for Jennifer at the desk. Colin was working at the front entrance computer. It seamed strange to me that although it has been over a month since they had seen Colin, they looked at him just as they had never seen him before. Colin was really intrigued as to why and how they would contact Jennifer, Colin put a call out for her as she went past, she winked at me as she walked up and talked to the two men, she smiled again, Colin thought to himself, I don't understand what's going on, but I will get to the bottom of this, you can be sure of that. While he was trying to over here them talking he couldn't here everything, so he tried getting nearer, each time he got nearer, thy moved further down the counter. Jacky-May was meant to meet Colin at the clinic at lunch time but it seemed, Colin had decided without telling anyone that he was going to follow these men again, and wasn't going to ask Jennifer to come with him this time, but Jennifer knew Colin so well. Colin followed the men out with a small package in each arm, he sneaked out thinking he wasn't seen, but Jennifer pulled up behind him and tooted her horn he jumped a mile! What a red face he had. Colin gets in your to obvious! She was laughing at him so much she forgot to keep an eye on the two men. Colin was furious at Jennifer and wanted to know what she was doing and who are the men?, Then! She said "don't you trust me now?" "I do, but what did you give them and how did they contact you"? "They sent an official looking document from a couple of labs, they are meant to be local? But when I rang the labs they didn't know what was going on? "So I thought we would follow them!" "You knew I was going to follow them, but why didn't you tell me?" lets just say women's intuition. "Let's stop talking and pick up Jacky-May, if we can" Colin replies Jacky-May knows as well! She laughed "you are easily surprised aren't you Colin"? "How did you organize this?" She just smiled at each other. It's all getting to Colin, all because he is used to being in control. But its exciting as well, not knowing what's going on from the moment you get up to the moment you go to bed. Colin had something he wanted to ask Jacky-May and asked Jennifer to stop at the pick nick area they had the pick nick the other day. She realised he wanted to ask Jacky-May to marry him, Jennifer was flabbergasted and didn't know what to say and blurted out "of-cause I will, she's getting a real nice guy, I knew she was under your skin Colin, but I can not believed you want to get engaged this soon"? Colin replied, "I realised that if anything after the storm, and Jacky-May nearly loosing her life, that I have to take the chance of a lifetime" "but of-cause you should, if that's the way you feel about her"? As they picked up Jacky-May Colin couldn't wait to ask her if she would marry him, so he asked her to get in the back of the car with him, and on the way to only Jennifer knows where? Colin blurted out "will you marry me?", there was a deadly silence from the shock that Jacky-May wasn't sure she heard him right? "what did you say Colin?" "Yes I asked you to marry me!", "yes! Yes! Yes! I will. Would you mind if I try and get in touch with my family to tell them? Although they are a bit over protective, I have them under control, since you did me the oner of phoning them, while I was in hospital, I have a lot to thank you for, and this is the best thing yet!" {and she gave him a long seductive kiss and said "you wait till where married, you hunk! As they got to the restaurant Jennifer explained "that there are police in the restaurant", "isn't she slick!" To slick for my liking thought Colin. We had followed them to an Italian restaurant, which again was prearranged. Jennifer explained there are a company of police on that table and the gangsters are over there on that table. Everything is being recorded for evidence of body-snatching. The group of police looked like a bunch of people celebrating a wedding anniversary. Jennifer said, "stay at this table you can see everything going on from here, and use it in your news paper. It could be a good scoop for you Colin! I will see you two after your dinner okay"? "You two will make a great couple and a great team, working together for the paper". She passed Colin a briefcase and said "this should be your next job Colin"? Jacky-May realised it was her briefcase and instantly said "where did you get this" "don't ask question's, Colin just study the case files you have there" Colin took a look and couldn't believe his eyes, there was all Jacky-May's folders and one of the contractors was old Mr Butterfield, Colin couldn't stop smiling, he had a great big cheesy grin from ear to ear, Jacky-May was surprised to have her briefcase back, Colin showed her the list of contractors and suppliers, and old Mr Butterfield so they all wanted Jacky-May out of the way. This brought Colin and Jacky-May closer together, they just held hands across the table, just as though they had won the jackpot on a $1000,000 bandit. Jennifer's knack of surprising them. She went over to another table and asked an man to dance with her Colin and Jacky-May watched them dancing and Colin asked Jacky-May to dance so they went up to dance. As they where dancing Jacky-May realised who Jennifer was dancing with, its the old man that brought the flowers to her, it put her in to a dream and it was then that she realised the old man was her real father, she remembers him passing her a dolly on her 4th birthday. She went over to the dance floor and asked Jennifer if she could dance with her dad, Jennifer just laughed and stepped to one side. Colin was wondering what was going on, he said to Jennifer "who is he?" He is her real father", you mean she was adopted"? "yes and you brought them together Colin. The flyers you had the police do, worked for them. "Anyway its back to work for me, thank you" said Colin and went back to the table to watch his true love dancing with the father she barely knew.

Colin looked over the papers in the briefcase and realised that when he was being followed by the to men in the jag, it was all because of old Mr Butterfield and his business dealings and nothing to do with the abortion's. He smiled to himself and couldn't wait to get to investigate the Butterfield's business dealings.

Back to the restaurant. Jacky-May introduced her farther and he sat talking a while and said to Colin and Jacky-May "you have a job to do, I'm proud of you Jacky-May! Good night I need my rest, see you soon." Jacky-May watched him leave in a white limousine, she was gob smacked to meat her real farther, and a few memories played back in her mind.

As they where sat at a good table for two and a romantic place it is. {Colin and Jacky-May just looked in to each others eyes, with a grin on there face's and starry eyed, they are definitely in love. Colin snapped out of it as Jennifer came over and talked to them. "Please take some photo's, when you two can stop holding hands and grinning like Cheshire cats will you Colin"? Of cause Colin agreed and {Colin always thought, he was good at taking pictures, but he will find out soon his Jacky-May has the talent of her own, much better than his picture taking, he will find she has a flair of picking the right angle with the light shimmering on her subjects!

Jennifer then suggested she better go to negotiate a deal for the remains? "We will call them" "okay, we understand, but they know you"? Yes I know but I got a friend to contact them after they called in at the clinic. Jacky-May said to Colin "we have a real detective here" "I wondered why she started helping us and took over maybe it was because she is a real copper after all"? Then she blushed and giggled. Colin suggested to Jacky-May to take some pictures", so she started snapping away taking plenty of Colin, he asked to look at them, and boy was he impressed with the way she used the light and laughed as he thought if only I had her talent, he was getting hungry and suggested they order a starter and the main course together "what would you normally eat at a place like this Colin?" "This place does the best Italian food for miles he suggested the spaghetti and meatballs for the main course, {that's only because Gran makes great meatballs and boy does he loves them}, but Jacky-May thought, she would try the linguine. In the middle of taking more pictures of Jennifer's meeting with the (body snatchers)and some of the police party. The police party really was in disguise, there was 6 couples, so it looked like a normal 60th anniversary party, they took plenty of photos, so I now these gangsters are going to jail, {go striate to jail, do not pass go, do not collect} LOL. Jacky-May said "its a shame what should be berried is sold to the highest bidder, to do scientific experiments!" "Yer but there's money in it, legally and illegally. Since the 1700 doctors have paid for bits of bodies, that's a part of the scientific culture, its all about the next breakthrough, and that also makes it all about money, the body-snatchers make and it goes to the highest bidder! Not just the experiments them selves. People will find anything that will make money! Jennifer got her men and they were charged with stealing bodies and selling them for profit, the courier wasn't charged with anything, as he really didn't know what he was transporting broke the law., one of Jennifer's favours, he got of with a caution.

THE CREATIVE NEWS.

BODY SNATCHER'S GOES AWAY FOR 25 YEARS EACH.

The two Body snatchers get 25years each for there dirty deeds of making money out of other peoples miseries, it was and is a sick thing to do to somebody's son or daughter. They showed no remorse for dealing in corpses, the judge said he had never seen such a case as disgusting as this one and gave them the maximum penalty. **Yours forever The creative writer.**

THE POLICE CATCH UP WITH DR RASHID.

They are trying to stop more people posing as doctors. And they are going to force a bill through the parliament to re-evaluate into ways to improve the system. Unfortunately there are those who would abuse the system; changing and regulating is not necessarily a robust immediate solution but a step forward in the right direction.

Yours thankfully **The creative writer**

THE CREATIVE NEWS PAPER.

The news about the ledger's abortionist. There was at the last count over 2059 illegal operations done by a rogue doctor. These were done by the lax doctor and surgeon Mr Rashid. Now in police custody for performing illegal operations and many accounts of murder are being sort by the police because of his misuse of his position of trust. He had duped people in to thinking he was a first class surgeon. He did unscrupulous abortions on children between the ages of 11 and 18.

Dr Rasead may have known the theory of being an abortionist, but his skill needed a lot to be desired, unfortunately we can only identify 2 years worth of patients as he was very efficient at getting rid of his records. He made over 2059 operations at the last count. The police have a lot of evidence to put him away for life. And there is still a lot of work to do, we need to Identify all of the patients that have been ill-treated by this person posing as a first class surgeon and doing a second class job. I am determined to find all these back street abortionists and doctors and bring them to account for there misuse of this country's doctor registration system which literally allows them to get away with murder. **Yours thankfully,The creative writer**

Proof Read by: Professor Nazrul Islam BEng Hons D32/D33 M.Inst.E

Author: Mr Terrence John FRY

Testimonial

'I Professor Nazrul Islam have enjoyed this book as an impressive piece of fiction. It is based on reality and a depiction of current issues. I wish the book to be given all the success and hope the avid readers will appreciate the depth of the core elements. It took him almost 7years its a great novelization for any to pick up and Read. Thank you ... ... Terry (T J FRY). Marvellous Old Boy!

ABOUT THE AUTHOR

Terrence John Fry has been a man who has been a good father with a moderate Christian upbringing. However, life as we know and share in reality brings trials and tribulations that out phase us from our own sensibilities.

He has come from humble upbringing's and shares a professional similitude with the proof reader who found him in a part of his life where things in life just seem over perplexed. It is then Terry understood what a wonderful father he is by an independent observation. Which brings me to highlight that if a man who has undergone the strife of betrayal from the inner circles it becomes therapeutic to novelise ones hardships in a way that can help others to achieve a far in depth intellectual stimulation by achieving the morals that are always intellectually challenging even when it is simplified.

Terrance J Fry is a honest kind human being that is relearning that life is precious more than we appreciate. We can not judge others based face value or shun any stigmas attached to the socio conventions that are perceived contradictory with the complexities of life.

Terrance J Fry is overcoming ones own calamities by an more realistic progressive non judgemental positive CREATIVE outlook!

Printed in the United States
By Bookmasters